Set Your Affections On Things Above

By

Ashan R. Hampton

ISBN 1-4033-4642-9 (e-book)
ISBN: 1-4033-4643-7 (Paperback)

This book is printed on acid free paper.

1st Books - rev. 10/02/02

ACKNOWLEDGEMENTS

❧

*What I tell you in darkness, that speak ye in light:
and what ye hear in the ear, that preach ye upon the
housetops. (Matthew 10:27 KJV)*

If ever I have written anything that I can truly deem divinely inspired, then this work, Set Your Affections On Things Above is that, of all that I have written, which truly deserves that distinction. Therefore I do not take credit for it, nor did I over the many months—early mornings, and sleepless nights—it took for me to write, longhand, the finished product you now hold. (Not to mention the numerous revisions!) I began to write this manuscript in the midst of one of the lowest, most isolating periods of my life; a time when I fiercely battled with myself, my issues and my God. In my natural strength, I could not have articulated the principles, the problems and spiritual solutions that lie in these pages. The good news is that I have become a more spiritual, settled, healed, free young woman, as a result of all that wrestling!

During the time when all of my single woman, man drama issues came to the fore, I could not find a book that discussed practical, spiritual living for women who desired to live holy and righteously in these perilous times. Instead, I found books on dating, mating and waiting, which did not discuss the purging and healing, the real touch from God that I needed. I truly believe that the Holy Spirit had me to live and to write the information I sought, to assist other women on their journeys to spiritual peace in the single life.

So, I give all thanks to the Father, Son and Holy Ghost—the Father, the creator of the universe, my spiritual covering; to Christ, my healer, savior and first husband, and to the Holy Spirit—my teacher and divine inspiration.

Since I did not include an acknowledgements page in my first published novel, Like She Knows Single, I would like to thank everyone by name, but that would be too prodigious a task!

However, I would like to thank my parents, Rita Faye and Charles Edward Hampton, and my sister Ahnna Alberta Hampton for supporting me when they did not fully understand me. My entire extended family—I don't want to make anyone mad or jealous by mentioning or omitting names! Eloise Fitzpatrick, Oshie Pledger, Beth Greenway and all the other numerous educators, church members and friends who participated in training me.

To Rev. William E. Thrasher, Jr., Rev. C. Earl Harvey, Betty Goodwin, Lucetta Jordan, Margaret Taylor, Rev. Jerry D. Black, Bishop Steven Arnold, Rev. Mark Seals, Rev. James Goolsby, Brother Kevin West, Evangelist Joanne Trammell, Prophetess Khadija Richardson, Ministers Milton Brown and Terry Jones, and Pastor and Sister Jones of Bethesda Apostolic Church in Little Rock, Arkansas for your strong spiritual leadership, prayers, counseling and friendship.

To all of my friends, both male and female, who commiserated and bore with me through all of my single woman, man drama; who inspired me and kept me company during all those local and long distance phone calls on many a dateless, manless weekend (or any other day when I was really feeling it!):

Marquelle Chapman, Meisha Finney Hall, LaShon Payne Hatton, Stephanie Jones, Nickey Ervin, Stacey Ellison, Adrian Nickyson, Oscar Joseph III, Santon Anderson, Roderick Jones, Kenneth Blair, Eric Griffin, Erica Mayes, Melanie Smith Williams, Jackie Smith, Danny Carter, Sam Richardson, Rick Walter, Darlene Givens, Sharese Willis, LaJuan Simpson, Kevin Lloyd, Kevin West, Horace Woods, Rodney Loveless, Brandon Massey, Erika Balfour, Deandrea Jones, Tammy Patterson, Norma Harris, Andrea Johnston, Kimberly Hendricks, Este Frazier, and Ariano Kei Moore.

To every guy Iive ever dated for any length of time, (or admired from afar) who brought me the fun, the drama and consequently the healing! May God bless your paths and bring you much love and success.

To the only two hairdressers I have ever had: Ms. Lois Profit of Little Rock, Arkansas and Ms. Mamie Johnson of Gainesville, Georgia.

Special thanks to Essie Lee Jackson, my grandmother, for all she was and still is in the hearts of my family. To my deceased good friend John Cannon from my Parkview Highschool days in Little Rock, Arkansas, who died much too young, but who knew me, loved me anyway, accepted me, and never let me forget my dreams. I have worked very hard over the years, especially since his passing, because I have never forgotten his.

Thanks for all of the lessons, love, support, prayers, well wishes, peace and blessings!

Dedication

❦

*This book is dedicated to everyone who has ever
laughed, talked, commiserated and cried with
me.
To those special ones who held me,
remembered me, and prayed for me.
To Jesus Christ who healed me,
and most graciously,
To the Holy Spirit who danced with me.*

Table of Contents

About the Author

Notes

About the Book

Unless otherwise quoted, all scripture quotations are taken from the New King James Version of the Bible. Copyright © 1979, 1980, 1982 by Thomas Nelson, Inc. Used by permission. All rights reserved.

Scripture quotations marked KJV are taken from the King James Study Bible, copyright 1988 by Liberty University.

Scripture quotations marked NIV are taken from the Holy Bible, NIV copyright © 1973, 1978, 1984 by the International Bible Society. Use of this trademark requires permission of the International Bible Society.

Scripture quotations marked NLT are taken from the Holy Bible, New Living Translation, Copyright ©1996. Used by permission of Tyndale House Publishers, Inc., Wheaton, Illinois 60189. All rights reserved.

INTRODUCTION

❧

IN THE BEGINNING

*Two are better than one, because they have a good
reward for their labor.
For if they fall, one will lift up his companion.
But woe to him who is alone when he falls,
For he has no one to help him up. (Ecclesiastes 4:9-
10)*

On the same day an attractive woman in my Sunday School class
announced her recent marriage, I had a long distance conversation
with my father who told me that a cousin of mine was going to be
married soon. "Well, good," I replied. "At least Honey (his mother)
will get to do somebody's wedding before this century is out."
Although this went unsaid, my dad and I were both secretly
wondering when it was going to be my turn and why I was not
attracting any prospects. After my 25th birthday, he reminded me that
even dogs and hobos ran in two's. At age twenty-eight, he

announced that he was going to buy another dog to serve as his surrogate grandchild.

As I assured my mother that I was indeed trying to keep the hope of meeting someone to marry alive, I jokingly told her, "Jesus is my boyfriend right now. I should get that printed on a T-shirt, so that when people ask why I am still single, I can just point to it." "Hey," she giggled, "I like that. Jesus is my boyfriend, and he should be. He should be like a husband, or someone personal to you." My mother and I laughed a bit more, but days later, I was still turning that amusing thought over in my mind. "Jesus is my boyfriend." This almost sounded defeatist, as if I had given up hope of ever snagging a mortal man and was settling into being an old maid (at twenty-eight) whom only Jesus could love.

However, the longer I thought about it, the concept of placing Jesus in this intimate context no longer seemed pathetic or sacrilegious to me. Thinking of Him in this way has allowed me to become clear on how my relationship with Jesus should function. Others have called Him the great love of their lives, their healer, the ultimate confidante or best friend, in order to fill the intimate void that existed in their individual lives at the time. For me, it was a boyfriend, or husband figure.

My emotional and spiritual aching place partly originated from my very ardent desire to experience the love of a man within a marriage for the purposes of shared spiritual growth and family. I had resolved in my mind that a man and marriage were absolutely necessary for me to experience the fullness of life and God's love for me.

A passionate marriage, a family oriented relationship, I further convinced myself, would allow me to completely love God, other people and aid me in being obedient to God. Marriage had freed so many others in those ways, so surely it also had to happen for me that way. But, it did not, in spite of all my efforts. And after a couple of years of praying, fussing, crying and claiming in His precious name, it still has not.

But then an extraordinary thing happened to me. After seeking God for what seemed to be a very long time, I received the strength to keep following Christ through tests of loneliness and depression that every single woman will endure.

However, before I received this life-changing gift from God, for several months, every Friday night, when I came in from work and felt the silence engulf me like an old familiar blanket, I cried. Cried and whined; cried and overate, until I fell asleep watching whatever was on *Nick at Nite* at the time. The weekends were difficult for me to bear, because wherever I went and all around me, couples were shuttling back and forth, sometimes hand in hand, yet I was alone.

I experienced visceral pangs of emptiness and jealousy whenever I heard someone announce a wedding or an engagement, or whenever I watched television and saw countless movies and commercials depicting men and women enjoying one another. I was a complete emotional mess internally, but no one could tell by my outward appearance. None of my co-workers, friends or family had any idea that on some days I didn't feel like getting out of bed, or that seemingly innocuous questions like "Are you dating anyone?"

nearly pushed me over the edge from being functionally to pathologically depressed.

You might ask, "All of this over the single life?" Although some married individuals might secretly wish to be single again, for many, single means unchosen and alone. This is unfortunately true for Black women who remain unmarried far longer than most women in America. A U. S. Census Report on the *Marital Status of Persons 15 Years and Over, by Age, Sex and Race* that was released in March 1998, reported that only 17.8 percent of white females and 24.3 percent of Hispanic women over 18 years had never been married. In comparison, 37.3 percent of Black females had not experienced their first marriage.[i] The fear of never acquiring a husband is not unreasonable for Black women, especially when the statistics and media portray the possibility of marriage for these women as being unlikely, or at best, rare.

I, like many other singles, have feverishly read several dating/relationship books written by Christian and secular authors alike. I tried to follow some of the advice that those books offered, such as,

Don't call him, get out of the house more often, engage in extracurricular activities that you typically would not, pray to God for your Divine mate, attend more church activities, etc., etc., all to no avail.

Over a period of about two years, I conscientiously tried some of these 'methods,' but none of them worked for me. However, in a last ditch effort to snag a man before my thirtieth birthday, against my better judgment and out of pure desperation, I bought a book called *The Sistah's Rules* by Denene Millner, which boasts of culturally specific dating rules for Black women. However, these ineffective 'rules' are presented with a carnal 'sistah girl' flavor. For example, Rule #1 is to "celebrate the power of the booty." I was embarrassed to admit that I had subjected my spirit to such trash, until I heard several other Christian girls confess that they had also purchased it. Reading these kinds of books only increased my frustration with the world's system of dating and mating. I soon realized that no information is as effective as the divine teaching and revelation of the Holy Spirit.

When I finally began to seek God's will for my life, or more accurately, after I screamed and cried and fussed at God, fell out on the floor and declared that God loved everybody except me, and granted everyone's petitions except mine, I discovered that what I really needed was more of God's presence in my life. Ultimately, my entire mate seeking drove me right into the arms of the one who loves me most.

Single women must realize that their incessant desires for love is God's call to seek Him first before considering marriage with a man who will never fill the space in their hearts that God has reserved for Himself. Therefore, praying to God for a husband whom He will have to compete with for your affection and attention is futile. Instead, the prayer should be for a cleansing of the soul that will enable God's love to manifest itself in your life in whatever form He chooses. I hope that every single woman who has bought or otherwise received this book will be inspired to seek her own revelation about the single life, intimacy with God and the sweet, transformative powers of the Holy Spirit.

Chapter 1

᪾

FUTURE HUSBANDS

For your Maker is your husband,
The Lord of hosts is His name...(Isaiah 54:5)

Many women have had boyfriends they thought would metamorphose into fiancées. He is usually that funny, smart guy they feel some ineffable connection to. The world calls this person a soul mate. In most cases, however, the longer the relationship progresses, the more difficult it becomes to break off, because the woman has allowed her soul (mind, will and emotions) to become tied to the man she desires. Fortunately, these carnal relationships with 'good' guys will always end, especially if God did not ordain the relationship. Sometimes the break ups are abrupt and emotionally ugly, because many times, women choose to ignore the

1

red flags along the way that indicate whether or not the relationship is truly of God's will, or selfish desires.

As a result, some women have experienced extended periods of heartache because they were unwilling to release the relationship when God impressed them to do so. In these cases the relationship will violently fall apart; the man will stop calling, or he will impregnate another woman. Regardless of the tactics used, God will force that unhealthy soul tie to be torn in an effort to save and heal both parties.

It seems that I was always meeting 'the guy' when I participated in the world's dating scene. One particular time, I met a young engineer that I was convinced was the one for me. He was tall, cute, twenty-five and already owned a house and a Lexus. I was excited at the prospects of sharing a life with him; traveling with him on business trips, attending corporate parties, cooking for him in his house.... my fantasies were endless. I was attracted to the idea of him providing me with the material amenities I could not provide for myself. For over a year, I allowed him to call and disappear. In the back of my mind, I knew there had to be another woman in his life. One night, he called me while on a business trip in Australia to confess his true feelings for me. I believed him when he said he wanted a more serious relationship with me. I danced around the apartment, happy that God had finally answered my prayers, since I had 'claimed' him as my husband a few months earlier. However, when I finally got in touch with him almost a month later, a girl answered his phone. He called back later to tactfully explain why a long-term relationship with me would not work after all.

For a long while after this episode, my emotions, ego and heart were bruised from the ups and downs, ins and outs of anticipating certain men as being my partner when it was not in God's plan for them to be. I, like many other women, permitted my flesh to pursue men who were emotionally and psychologically unavailable to me. It took a while for me to figure out why this cycle of 'meet and dismiss' kept occurring in my life.

The answer is in II Corinthians 6:14, which says, "Do not be unequally yoked together with unbelievers. For what fellowship has

3

righteousness with lawlessness? And what communion has light with darkness?" This passage of scripture is often quoted to single people as advice to follow when considering potential partners, but its veracity is applicable to the dating and relationship practices that many Christian women have adopted. For example, in attempts to fulfill the "get out of the house" requirement for meeting Mr. Right, some women frequent places where few Godly men can be found, such as Christian clubs, house parties, card games, or sports bars. On the other hand, some women only attend church functions, but their skirts are too short, dresses too tight and blouses are cut too low. I have actually heard women admit that they have provocatively positioned themselves to catch the attention of a deacon or minister in the pulpit. Unfortunately, there are plenty of beautiful women warming the church pews Sunday after Sunday who are utterly embarrassed to discuss the measures they have employed to find a mate.

The news and print media are partly responsible for provoking this type behavior by inundating women with information to demonstrate how dismal the institution of marriage has become. The media's fascination with high profile divorces and adulterous affairs has diminished the prospects of marriage for many women. Black women in particular have been told that most Black men are either in jail, or gay. Successful men like Wesley Snipes and Dennis Rodman have publicly declared their refusal to date Black women in favor of Asian and Caucasian women. These detestable facts make finding a partner a particularly pressing concern for many Black women. Unfortunately, these incessant messages from hell have prompted many Christian women to adopt the world's thoughts about relationships and how to pursue them.

It is sad to see how loneliness and depression have wounded and destroyed so many precious Black women. Black women who have been mistreated, abandoned, or ignored by men force themselves to live without the hope of experiencing a great love relationship. However, trying to live outside the boundaries of love is like trying to love Christ outside of the Holy Spirit. No fruit will develop and a

5

potentially ripe, rich experience will become a barren seed in the hostile field of the believer's heart.

Loneliness, depression, fear and low self-esteem have rendered many Black women struggling single parents, unhappy divorcees, middle-aged bachelorettes and corpses. To escape these fates, Black women have listened to the counsel of the unGodly, with regard to finding a husband. Unfortunately, the pray and wait on the Lord technique might cut into their best childbearing years. God might want them to remain single until age 35, and then He might choose an unappealing little man with a really good heart rather than the six-foot, chocolate Apollo they had in mind. (Oh yes, aren't we all familiar with these justifications to snag a man by any means necessary?)

When seeking God becomes a priority in a woman's life, the world becomes increasingly dissatisfying. She will begin to hunger for a different way to conduct her daily life. Women who decide to stop vacillating between the world and the Kingdom, between clubs and church, will find it more difficult to operate according to worldly systems, because their thoughts will begin to change. Many single women begin to notice these changes best when old relationships stop working, or the man they thought would 'rescue' them from loneliness does not.

Spiritual Christian women will not feel comfortable in nightclubs, bars, or other places where people are drunk with wine and not with the Holy Ghost. Unfortunately, many carnal Christians find it difficult to break these old patterns of behavior, especially when they are new in the faith. Some of my female friends still go to clubs with the intentions of meeting men. Needless to say, I cannot talk with them, or spend time with them socially like I used to, because they have not made the decision to live the life of holiness that Christ has called us to.

Romans 13:13 clearly states, "Let us walk honestly, as in the day; not in rioting and drunkenness, not in chambering and wantonness, not in strife and envying." Christians are to live life uprightly, not according to the lewdness of the flesh, or the merrymaking (rioting) that people often engage in at clubs and bars. Many women have frequented these "pick up spots" out of desperation to find a companion, but spiritually mature men will not be found in those places. Having a mature relationship with Christ is key, because we are living in a time when people profess to be Christians, but live carnal lifestyles. Such hypocrisy is unacceptable in the sight of our holy God.

Many of you are getting tired of looking and are upset with God for not allowing you to marry or have children before age thirty like you had planned. College, job, family is still the sequence that parents and friends expect you to follow. If you have fallen short of the third phase—family (regardless of your age) - you might begin to question if this is in God's plan for you. At this point of questioning, it is very easy for satan to overwhelm your soul with loneliness and depression. You must quickly counter this attack with thoughts of God's promises and love for you.

When I decided to find my own husband like everyone else did in clubs, gas stations, and through dating services, I felt uncomfortable and became depressed about always coming up empty-handed. This is what happens when we try to work outside of God's will and guidance. Psalms 16:11 declares, "Thou wilt show me the path of life: in thy presence is fullness of joy; at thy right hand there are pleasures for evermore" (KJV).

If you ask God for guidance in every aspect of your life, even in relationships, He will provide the peace you need to follow the blueprint that He has drawn especially for you. Does it take some time to finally get to this point of consulting God about what you are to do with your life? Yes! Before I finally surrendered my desire to marry to God, I experienced the pits of loneliness and depression that the single life can catapult even the most Christ-centered people into. I felt unloved and unchosen and these feelings nearly overtook me.

Once while in the midst of one of my 'moments,' I thought God was punishing me with singleness, until I became reacquainted with an old friend who in my opinion surpassed all other guys as future partners. We both thrived on provocative ideas, creativity, the pursuit of knowledge and absolutely enjoyed talking to one another. All of these qualities were highly important to me in a mate.

He seemed to be my soul mate. One night, toward the end of a deeply intimate conversation, he said the words I had longed to hear a guy say to me, "I have never felt for anyone else the way I feel about you." I was elated. I prayed that God would just go ahead and open the way for him to move to Georgia and fall madly in love with me, but I did not hear from that friend again until more than one year later. I called and e-mailed, but he never responded.

I got mad at him, God, and myself. How could my friend have said that to me, then refuse to communicate with me any more? How could God have sent this kindred spirit my way then allow him to go another direction, probably after some less than compatible female? Why did this situation keep repeating itself in my life? I internalized all of this anguish, because I was embarrassed to discuss my pain with friends or family.

Many feel that loneliness and depression are fairly innocuous issues that can be easily overcome by making the effort to do something, but if you are doing that 'something' alone, then feelings of loneliness rightfully exacerbate. Sometimes, you get tired of taking yourself to the movies and these feelings are valid. But then, you might begin to feel guilty for indulging in self-pity over something as inconsequential as being single when others have suffered trials much more severe. Entertaining feelings of guilt is dangerous, because it estranges you from God and puts you in mental bondage.

Therefore, it is better to honestly acknowledge what you feel and tell God that you need to be released from these turbulent emotions that are affecting your relationship with Him. A bruised, broken-hearted person has a difficult time experiencing the love and closeness of God. That is why in fulfilling the prophetic word of Isaiah, Jesus says, "The Spirit of the Lord is upon Me, because He has anointed me to preach the gospel to the poor; He has sent me to heal the brokenhearted, to proclaim liberty to the captives and recovery of sight to the blind, to set at liberty those who are oppressed" (Luke 4:18).

Christ has given us His spirit to not only comfort us, but to heal our broken hearts and bruised emotions. For many, the search for a husband or broken relationships have caused great pain that has formed walls around their hearts that God must penetrate in order to commune with them the way He desires to. Nothing can come before God and our relationship with Him. That includes nursing old wounds, which causes us to indulge in behaviors or emotions that are contrary to the peace and love of God. In effect, we tend to want to take care of our pain before having a relationship with God, which actually blocks Him from being able to fully abound within our hearts.

We must be healed first before we can fully experience God. I had to be emotionally healed. At first I was embarrassed to admit this to myself, as some of you might. I had sung the song "Jesus Loves Me" as a child, but as an adult, I had to admit that I was not feeling the love. I was prompted by the Spirit to repeat the following scripture to myself whenever satan tried to make me think that I was too far removed from God for Him to love me:

Yea, I have loved thee with an everlasting love: therefore

with lovingkindness have I drawn thee (Jeremiah 31:3 KJV).

After understanding God's love for me, I realized that my spiritual development would have been stunted in a relationship with my 'soul mate.' In hindsight, God did me a great favor by severing the soul tie that existed between us.

If you desire to be released from searching for love in all the wrong places, or from people who cannot and will not give it to you, then offer a prayer to God asking Him to break down the walls of pain your broken heart has erected to protect itself. This is a powerful first step in allowing the Holy Spirit to be released into your life.

Dear God, In the name of Jesus, I come before

you today with an open heart, asking that you

fill it with the love you have for me.

I have been so hurt and disappointed in past relationships

that did not fulfill my needs for companionship or love

like I thought they would.

Your word states that you have loved me with an

everlasting love, and I pray to enter into your divine,

loving presence right now to be healed and made whole

by your Spirit that is always surrounding me.

May I feel and always be reminded of the divine love you

have for me.

In Jesus' name I thank God that is done,

Amen.

Chapter 2

∽

FIGHTING THE CLOCK

He shall be like a tree planted by the rivers of water,
That brings forth its fruit in its season;
Whose leaf also shall not wither;
And whatever he does shall prosper. (Psalms 1:3)

"Girl, if we're going to get married then we have to leave Atlanta.

The men here are not thinking about marriage, and they are no good.

Trust me, I've been here six years and haven't found a good one yet;

that's why I'm getting ready to move somewhere where the ratio of

women to men is better." A female friend that I met in a salsa dance

class and I would have 'amen' discussions like that all the time, until

she found a boyfriend, and left me in the dust. I have heard and

overheard similar stories from Black women who find themselves

being strung along by men with less than honorable intentions, and

Black men who claim that most women are materialistic and lousy

15

cooks. When I ran out of people to complain to about the single life, I developed a web page where other frustrated singles could vent and receive encouragement, but after getting a few thousand hits, visits to the page lessened.

I found that some who visited the page basically thought I was a frustrated woman who needed to get a grip and get a life. Well, insensitive people who are in relationships easily give that advice to singles, especially married couples who do not realize the perils of singleness in this day and time. For example, it seemed that no matter how dysfunctional the relationship some of my female friends were in, that in some sense they still felt superior to me and other women, since they obviously had no trouble getting men, regardless of the <u>quality</u> of those men.

They would send me e-mails on subjects like dating tips that were only addressed to the 'single gals.' Interestingly enough, although I was dealing with my own issues about being single, I crossed paths with a variety of males and females with similar experiences that I wound up encouraging and giving advice to.

Unfortunately, I have met too many young women under thirty who are involved in unequally yoked, live-in relationships. Many of them have become single mothers, because they were willing to compromise their values to avoid the frightening prospect of growing older without a man in their lives.

Despite the decayed morals and high divorce rate in this country, there is still the expectation of women to marry before thirty, although new trends show that people are marrying later in life, well after they have become established in their careers. This might be true, but women still struggle against the "old maid," woman on the corner with ten cats in her yard, stereotype that was indoctrinated in the psyche of Americans many years ago. For example, it was once reported that a woman over thirty had a better chance of being kidnapped by a terrorist than to marry.

Because the secular media has painted such a dismal picture of relationships, many Black women feel that they might never find a mate. Even Christian women have bought into this mentality, and as a result, they have begun to doubt that God will indeed supply all of their emotional and sexual needs. They express this doubt by joining dating services, or posting personal ads on the Internet. They often excuse this faithless behavior by convincing themselves that by using 'Christian' matchmaking services or web sites that they are not really infringing upon God's plans for their lives. The root of all this behavior and thinking is fear - the fear that God, the creator of the universe, will not consider this need for companionship important enough to provide the best mate possible for those who desire a partner.

When the single life gets a little tough to bear, my friends and I use free long distance minutes and e-mail to find comfort in one another. "Can we really be okay without men?" we ask. We begin to empower ourselves by thinking of the sweet, bleary eyed martyrs we so often see chasing their children through the aisles, or spanking their little hands to cease their incessant importuning. They wear sweats in every color of the rainbow, with their hair pulled back into a ponytail, or some other tacked up fashion, because they have no time to maintain that sense of style they had before they sacrificed their lives to their families.

When they stand, we see the hip that has supported their little ones for so long bend slightly to the left or right, and declare to ourselves that no man will initiate the premature ruin of our cute little bodies. Despite our attempts to diminish the importance of having a family by looking at married women who seem to be having a bad time of it, we still envy the fact that they do not have to enter an empty apartment with no other human voices present except those streaming through the television.

It seems that the closer I get to thirty, the more concerned my parents become about my single status, although they would never admit that aloud. Some of their friend's daughters have already gotten married, (and are near divorce), and have produced grandchildren. My father says pretty soon I will be too old to think about having children and that I should look into buying my own house, since I won't have a man or a family to consider. My mother says she prays daily that the right man will enter my life. After sharing their sentiments with other single females, I have found that they also get pressed by their parents to complete the sequence: college, job, marriage and kids. If this is the case, then single women are only half complete and are running out of time!

Sometimes, we need to be reminded that our will and efforts cannot supersede God's. This is the difference between living by faith, and according to the limited resources of the world. As believers, we have enough faith to know that God does not have the same concept of time that we have, and will not allow us to alter His plans for our lives. We often frustrate the plan, wander into the wilderness, and make an eleven day trip to the promised land take years to complete (Deuteronomy 1:2). However, if we continue to seek His guidance, we will experience the fullness of life the way God intended us to.

For example, Sarah thought God was mistaken, or didn't realize how old she was when He told her and Abraham that they would bear a son. Her biological clock had stopped ticking a long time before God spoke to them, in her opinion. In fact, when she heard the news, she laughed inwardly at the idea of Abraham having those kinds of 'relations' with her, considering how old they were, just as Abraham had when God initially spoke this promise to him (Genesis 18:10-15). Sarah frustrated God's plan and caused both of them to enter the wilderness when she brought Hagar into their lives (Genesis 16), but God, in His infinite grace and mercy, opened Sarah's womb and blessed them with Isaac whom God needed to be born of Sarah, not Hagar, in order for His will to be fulfilled on earth.

Sarah's barrenness was a thorn in her side, just like singlehood is for many women, because her innermost desire was to bear children, just as it is for some to marry and have a family. In fact, in myriad cultures down through the ages, it was dishonorable and shameful for women to not bear children, especially sons, or to remain single, and these archaic ideas have been passed down throughout the collective unconscious to affect our modern attitudes toward marriage and family. Nonetheless, Sarah knew that God had told Abraham that he would be the father of many nations, but as of her ninetieth birthday, Sarah had still not born any children. As a result of her human reasoning, she devised an alternate plan, just as I did when I tried all those dating 'methods.'

I know that God does not wish for man to live alone (Genesis 2:18), but when I attend wedding and baby showers, it seems that He has forgotten that I, a *wo*-man, am still without a mate. However, if I continue to live my life by faith, acting like I know God is God and is faithful to his people (Deuteronomy 7:9), and do not upset his plans for me by trying to buy, create, or otherwise influence a man to marry me, then I, and my parents, will live to see the day when I walk down the aisle and say, "I do."

I wish I could tell you that I immediately found solace in these revelations but I did not, not completely. I had good days and bad days. During this time, I still managed to socialize with people instead of walling myself up within my apartment. I went to work, took a belly dancing class, took up salsa dancing, continued to take myself out on dates, and ate chocolate on my 'bad' days.

True contentment only comes when you decide to trust God by releasing your entire life and soul - mind, will and emotions - to His divine intentions for your time on earth, all the while confessing the word in Jeremiah 29:11, "For I know the thoughts that I think toward you, says the Lord, thoughts of peace and not of evil, to give you a future and a hope." Your complete surrender and faith in His goodness will make it easier to trust God, His timing and the plans He has for your life.

> *Dear God,*
>
> *I come before your divine throne of grace and mercy,*
> *asking that my mind and concept of time be released to that*
> *of Christ's.*
> *Forgive me for the things I have done and wrong words of*
> *faithlessness*
> *I have spoken in trying to make things occur in my life*
> *according to my timing and not God's.*
>
> *Your word says that you know the thoughts you think*
> *toward me, and that they are of peace.*
> *Help me to accept the wonderful plan you have designed for*
> *me,*
> *that will unfold in the fullness of your divine timing,*
> *flowing with the blessings you surely have in store for me.*

In Jesus' name I pray and thank you that it is done.

Amen.

Chapter 3

∽

COME CLOSER

Draw near to God, and he will draw near to you.
(James 4:8)

During one of my 'episodes,' I told God, out of mild frustration, that I couldn't really hear what He was trying to say to me and the words "come closer" very gently came to my spirit. At first, I questioned whether or not that was really God and not just one of my random thoughts. I expected Him to be a little less laconic by sending a barrage of quotable, lyrical words to my conscience.

Although this phrase was not as poetic as I had imagined, I knew it was God dealing with me in straight forward, unsugar-coated truth, in accordance with the scripture in Hebrews 4:12, "For the word of God is quick and powerful and sharper than any two-edged sword, piercing even to the dividing asunder of soul and spirit and of the joints and marrow, and is a discerner of the thoughts and intents of the heart" (KJV).

At the time I heard the phrase, "come closer," I knew that I had not been praying or studying the Bible as consistently as I should have been, although I knew that I would never become intimate with God without developing good habits in these areas. Prayer allows us to communicate with God, but God reveals Himself to us through His word. Although God deals with people through dreams, visions, prophets and a variety of other ways, most often, revelation knowledge comes primarily through the consistent study of scripture. By telling me to come closer, God was admonishing me to stabilize my faith by talking to Him through prayer and learning His true character by studying the scripture.

Single women must realize that building a relationship with God is a process; one with extremely high reward, but not without its bumps and bruises. Hard heads and bruised egos will constantly need to be dealt with and brought under the control of the Holy Spirit. However, it is important not to become discouraged in your walk with Christ when you make mistakes, or when it seems that your life is falling apart.

It takes determination and courage to plow ahead believing that moving forward with God has to be much better than all the mess and condemnation you have left behind. I could not go back to the worldly pit I was in; it was much too terrible. So I began to trust that God was directing my path, because I was no longer using the road map I had created for my life. Mark 11:22 says, "Have faith in God," but in reality, keeping the faith is not always easy, because giving up control to God is uncomfortable and scary to the natural mind. Therefore, in order to establish solid footing in our lives, we have a tendency to revert to our old plans when we cannot fully understand where God is leading us.

Some have been taught that having faith in God means they will completely understand God's plans and will always be comfortable following God in all situations. On the contrary, scripture shows us through the likes of Noah, Abraham, Gideon and Ezekiel that God will make us do things that make no earthly sense. In fact, following

God in faith will sometimes make us appear foolish in the eyes of unbelievers or carnal Christians. By considering these biblical examples, it seems that we begin to walk in faith when we overcome fear, abandon human reasoning, the need to understand, and begin to trust that God's ways are perfect and will not lead us into harm.

However, when our faith is tested, it is difficult to hear God when we focus on our circumstances rather than God's sovereignty. During times of struggle, it is natural for us to want to immediately fix the problem. As a result, we are prone to make decisions without consulting God first. Realizing the error of our ways can make us feel guilty for not trusting God to handle the situation, which can further make us question whether or not we truly have faith in God.

Every time I regressed into old habits, even if for a moment, satan tried to make me feel condemned for doing so by distorting the message in Romans 1:8, "There is therefore no condemnation to them which are in Christ Jesus, who walk not after the flesh, but after the Spirit." I was made to feel as if I did not qualify for Christ's covering, since I had pursued the flesh in my regressions. One of satan's strategies for your defeat is to make you feel that it is impossible to rise above the flesh to truly live according to God's word, but the Bible, especially the New Testament, clearly debunks this fallacy.

This is what real spiritual growth feels like. Many concentrate on the promises of God without considering the struggle. Removing yourself from the world's system to follow God's spiritual laws is a constant battle, and is highly uncomfortable to the flesh, especially in the beginning; "but we glory in tribulations also: knowing that tribulation worketh patience; And patience, experience; and experience hope" (Romans 5:3-4 KJV). In the New King James Version of the Bible, "patience" is translated as "perseverance" and "experience" as "character."

The process of spiritual growth is experienced, as outlined in the above scripture, when building a true love relationship with Christ. Jesus clearly tells us in scripture that His followers will become enemies to the world and to the prince of this world. As a result, we, as Christians, will face discomfort and even tragedy in our lives on earth. Whereas these experiences could destroy an unbeliever, for a submitted Christian, they serve to develop the patience and perseverance necessary to withstand the struggle.

During the "experience" part of the continuum is where slight regressions to old behaviors and thought patterns occur, because Christ is trying to press His fruit, which is His character, into us. After all of this, "Hope," reminds us to continually expect God to deliver us and remain faithful to His promises. The verse of a song that has become a 'churchy' expression, "Please be patient with me. God is not through with me yet," certainly holds true as you find yourself getting increasingly better, but never perfect. We will never be fully perfected until Jesus returns and we receive our glorious, new spiritual bodies. Until then, we must always allow our physical and spiritual vessels to be purged and sanctified, pressing on toward fulfilling the call, or the mission that God has established for us.

HOW TO DEVELOP INTIMACY WITH GOD

The first thing I began to do when I resolved to build intimacy with Jesus was to study the Bible and seek information from spiritually inspired books, tapes, and television broadcasts. You cannot expect to hear from God if you do not abide in His Word on a consistent basis. Consistency and discipline have always been difficult for me to develop. Inconsistency is the reason why sometimes I can see definition in my abs and sometimes I can't, because I fluctuate from working out regularly to not at all. Since I desire to be led by the Holy Spirit in all situations, I have made it a point to surround myself with music, or some source of contact with the message of God's Word, several times throughout the day.

The book *The Love Every Woman Needs: Intimacy With Jesus*, by Jan McCray, blessed me in my initial attempts to "come closer" to God. From this book, I learned the terminology of "the aching place" to articulate the immense emotional void that I desperately needed Christ to fill. There was truly a hurting place in the core of my being that could not be excised or ameliorated by anyone but Jesus. Joyce Meyer, in the mini-book *Tell Them I Love Them*, says that there is a God-shaped hole in all of us that only He can fill, and I found this to be abundantly true.

The studying and praying I had begun to do went well for a while, until it seemed that what little I had in this world to hang on to was subject to crumble. Once again, I felt depressively low in spirit, because I did not understand that satan brings the most opposition when you resolve to follow God no matter what. However, on the flip side, when God is purging the junk from your life so that the Holy Spirit can abide in you more fully, you will likewise feel depressed, especially when God separates you from old comforts and pleasures you became attached to in the flesh.

While experiencing the double whammies of God's purification and satan's oppression, nothing made me happy. There was nothing in life to smile about and I felt like the walking dead. I remember walking into the house from having run some errand feeling absolutely exasperated. I needed to feel the love of God, so I read Jeremiah 31:3 again, then I picked up McCray's book, but put it right back down. I flipped on the television and went to the kitchen to get something to eat.

Benny Hinn was opening his show by discussing God's love for people. He looked right into the camera and very forcefully said, "You, you, you," and with each emphasis the camera zoomed in on a headshot, so that his face completely filled the screen. "Yes, you lady, right there, God is talking to you, with long dark hair. He says He has not forgotten about you and the situation you are dealing with right now. God loves you." Well, of course satan said that he could have been talking to a million ladies with long dark hair. It was just a fluke that I have long dark hair, and it was probably an older, pre-recorded show anyway; therefore, scores of women had probably already heard that broadcast and assumed he was giving a message to them.

I circumvented satan's mental attack by choosing to receive that word, at which point I bawled and <u>praised</u> God, rather than whine. Afterward, I splashed cold water on my face and finished eating. I have had to resist falling into the pit of despair many times since then. Although you will stumble and have your moments of doubt on this journey, God will provide you with the strength you need to be brought to completeness. "I can do all things through Christ which strengtheneth me" (Philippians 4:13 KJV) has become a mantra for me during these times of struggle. It is amazing how quickly repeating the word of God can settle your heart with peace.

A person who has been convicted of sin, and has truly entered the presence of God, realizes how Holy He is, and how grossly unclean the natural self is. Many have felt like filthy rags while asking for forgiveness, but the word reminds us that Jesus is able "to present [us] faultless before the presence of His glory with exceeding joy" (Jude v. 24). God is more than happy to welcome us into His presence and love.

To remind myself of this truth, I began to repeat the part of Jeremiah 31:3 that reads, "...I have loved thee with an everlasting love: therefore with lovingkindness have I drawn thee," whenever the devil tried to make me question God's genuine and eternal love for me. As a result, I soon began to notice changes in my behavior and mindset. Although I had not attained the spiritual nirvana others spoke of, I did have a lot more peace and clarity than I had before.

Despite all of the spiritual work I had surrendered to, some things about being single still perturbed me, and still do. Sometimes when I see couples enjoying one another, either in public or on television, I feel a little pang, not of jealousy, but of urgency for God to hurry up and send a man my way. Love songs that celebrate relationships bother me a bit, but I'm okay. People still tell me that I will find someone when I am not looking and I internally counter with, "Seek and ye shall find, knock and it shall be opened unto you" (Matthew 7:7 KJV).

At this point in my singleness, I still had not run out of good ideas yet. It dawned on me that I had not fervently and specifically prayed for a husband. So I prayed according to the word of God for a husband. Eventually, I stopped praying that 'marriage prayer' and began to believe that it was already done. Besides, I finally got tired of whining about being mateless and tried to move on.

Before I got to that point, however, I did what many of us have probably done in the past; made a list of all the characteristics I wanted my mate to have. In fact, in the next chapter, I will share an excerpt from the "Marriage Prayer" I developed while I was in the midst of trying all those dating 'methods' that were sure to snag me a man. The prayer might look familiar to some of you. Hopefully, you will also be encouraged to settle your longings to be married with God, as you continue to read what has been revealed to me about singlehood and marriage.

Before you read the entertaining marriage prayer I actually wrote and prayed a few years ago, first pray that whatever is keeping you from drawing near to God will be removed from your life. Praying this prayer might mean that some people, habits, or objects that once brought you pleasure must be removed, but have faith that all things are working for your good, and for the relationship you desire to have with God.

Heavenly Father,
I thank you and praise you for the enlightenment that
I am receiving concerning my life and relationship with
you.

Lord, I am committed to following your ways and to having

your spirit released in my life.

Therefore, I pray for the strength to release my attachment to everything in my life that is hindering me from drawing closer to you.

In Jesus' precious name, I pray and thank God that it is done.

Amen.

Chapter 4

৵ঌ

THE MARRIAGE PRAYER

Therefore a man shall leave his father and mother and
be joined to his wife, and they shall become one flesh.
(Genesis 2:24)

Some of the 'requests' I delineated for my future husband are cosmetic, but the majority of them reflect some degree of spiritual maturity. I tried to include traits that would not only satisfy my physical desires, but those that would foster professional and spiritual development between my husband and me. I certainly giggled a time or two as I reread the entire list, recalling the circumstances and state of mind I was in when I constructed this litany of characteristics for my future mate. I sometimes refer back to this list when examining the men that cross my path that I think could be 'the one' God has sent. (Just to make sure.)

Please God note that these requests are not in any specific order, or in order of importance, because all of them are important!

1. A man who knows how to pray, depend on God and attends church where the pastor, word and works of the church are anointed and ordained by God.

2. Let my partner have a good, attractive spirit; a spirit that is loving, Christ-centered and heals the heart and emotions. Let him make me feel special, loved and cared for.

3. Writes or appreciates good poetry and literature; my marriage partner has to be a man that will understand and challenge me intellectually.

4. Let him be a professional; either in my field of English or a fellow professor in any field, or a professional in a corporate or work environment who is successful and who still has an interest and appreciation for my work.

5. A man who thinks I am great just the way I am and will not try to change me.

6. He has no excess baggage. I do not want to raise anyone else's children or have to deal with deranged ex-wives or girlfriends.

7. A man who will clean the shower, keep the toilet seat down (or will not object to performing this courtesy) and will share the housework with no argument.

8. Adding this man to my life will not disrupt my peace, or hinder future plans for my life.

9. A wise leader who makes sound, spiritual decisions; has no outstanding debts; is not given to riotous living; in the age range of mid to late 20's to 35.

10. Tall, six feet or over and has a good build for his size.

11. He will respect my feelings on celibacy, but will be with me and no other woman even while we are dating.

12. Someone who is ready to marry and does not believe in long engagements; six months maximum or less if we are truly meant for each other.

13. That he is honest and shows his goodness to God, others and me.

Do you think this man exists? Sometimes I think that God will have to supernaturally create this man for me, but hey, nothing is too hard for God! I firmly believe I John 5:14, which reads, "Now this is the confidence that we have in Him, that if we ask anything according to His will, He hears us." Of course the key phrase in this verse is "<u>His</u> will."

Lists like these will undoubtedly be adjusted according to the lessons learned while developing an intimate relationship with Jesus. For example, if I were to revise this list now, I would blatantly list the fruit of the Holy Spirit found in Galatians 5:22-23, "But the fruit of the Spirit is love, joy, peace, longsuffering, gentleness, goodness, faith, Meekness, temperance (self-control): against such there is no law" (KJV).

Although you should not restrict God to your own valuations of a good mate, developing lists like this will help you to get clear on your current perceptions of a potential marriage partner. And if they are warped or otherwise skewed, get ready for the Holy Spirit to reveal your issues and God's truth in a big way, then write what He has taught you, and compare His list against yours!

While I was actively dating, I did not restrict myself to guys with certain physical characteristics, therefore, except for height, none appear in the marriage prayer. However, as humans, we have certain aesthetic preferences that we should not necessarily condemn ourselves for having (unless they are obsessive, restrictive or ridiculous). I have heard women jokingly say things like, "I could be looking for tall, dark and handsome when God wants to send me short, fair and mildly attractive." Actually, statements like these are problematic because the underlying idea is that God will give you an inferior gift. (A husband is a gift from God and should be revered as such). While it is true that God's thoughts and ways are higher than ours, to the extent that we often ask out of ignorance, Psalm 37:4 promises that God will give us the desires of our heart, but only if we delight ourselves in Him first.

I firmly believe that God will match me with someone who is not only compatible with me spiritually, but mentally, sexually and intellectually as well, so as not to be "unequally yoked" (II Corinthians 6:14). In regards to my mate, I told a friend that God would totally hook me up! Never fear that you and God will have polarized opinions concerning your life and mate. When you truly submit to God's authority, your desires become aligned with His.

A WOMAN OF GODLY CHARACTER

Making lists such as these is not necessarily a bad thing. Let us not forget the one that the wise King Solomon provides in Proverbs 31:10-31, the passage of the "virtuous woman." After having had many experiences with women (700 wives and 300 concubines), these are the characteristics that he deemed important for a Godly wife to have. In fact, it is most interesting to read the advice Solomon gives to men about women throughout the book of Proverbs.

Some of the warnings are hysterical! For example, Proverbs 21:19 (KJV) says, "It is better to dwell in the wilderness than with a contentious and an angry woman." It seems that Solomon had good knowledge of women with bad attitudes, because there are several verses that advise men against getting involved with incendiary women. For example, verse nine of that same chapter says, "It is better to dwell in a corner of the housetop, than with a brawling woman in a wide house." Needless to say, if you have termagant potential, it is imperative that you allow God to do an overhaul on your personality before you can expect to have a good husband!

Instead of citing each verse within this passage, I have used contemporary language to summarize the characteristics that each verse extols. According to Proverbs 31:10-31, a virtuous woman is:

*emotionally supportive (11)

*a blessing by acting well toward her husband, not a curse (12)

*industrious and willing to work (verses 13, 14, 17)

*willing to rise early and cook for the family (15)

*a wise businesswoman who is able to 'close shop' even if it extends to late evening hours (16, 18)

*able to sew and is an industrious worker (19)

*willing to serve others beyond her family (20)

*able to prepare the household for potentially lean times, like winter (21)

*able to make tapestries and fine clothing for herself, or otherwise economically resourceful and creative (22)

*the partner of a respected man in the community (23)

*financially enterprising (24)

*strong, honorable and light-hearted (25)

*able to give wise counsel and speak with love (26)

*willing to work to keep the house in order and is not lazy (27)

*a woman who makes her children and husband proud of her (28)

*the 'cream of the crop' amongst other women (29)

*a woman whose relationship with God determines her suitability versus physical beauty (30)

*a reaper of the good fruit of her labors that will be honored by God in heaven (31)

Well, ladies. Based upon these biblical criteria, are you a woman of Godly character? If you pale in comparison to this portrait of a virtuous woman, then are you truly ready to serve God and your husband in a marriage? In order to determine wife readiness, it is important for women to gauge their personality and character against these God inspired qualities. Doing so will undoubtedly make us less apt to create long laundry lists of characteristics we want our mates to possess.

Just as Solomon surely constructed the characteristics of a virtuous woman later in life when he was better able to examine his past relationships with wiser and more spiritual eyes, I constructed that list after I had gained more experience with God and men, but not <u>spiritual</u> men. I had indeed prayed for a husband and I met one. Someone <u>else's</u> husband, and I did not find that humorous at all.

I later surmised that God was telling me that I was not ready to have my own husband, and that I still needed to perceive men and relationships through spiritual senses, instead of the natural. However, to remain on the safe side, whenever I do mention something to God about the person I am going to marry, I make it clear that I am referring to the man that will be <u>my</u> very own man whom God has chosen to marry me and me only!

DETERMINING WIFE READINESS

I thought I was ready to be a wife, until I had to answer this very crucial question, just as all of us must: **"How is your relationship with Jesus Christ?"** For me, answering this question enlightened me on things about myself that I had not considered, which were not relative to my looks or personality. I was forced to understand and practice the spiritual principles that are integral to having a good relationship with the Savior.

The Holy Spirit asked me to consider additional questions like, *Have you told Him how much you love Him? Have you been faithful in your affections by cherishing Him above all else, such as cars, kids, and job? Have you been out on a date with God lately? Do you discuss your day or major decisions with Him?*

When I looked more closely at the nature of these questions, after I had to honestly answer each one, it became clear to me that the Holy Spirit had placed God in a context that I could humanly understand. Since I somewhat understood what it meant to have a solid relationship with a man, I used those same principles to understand how my personal relationship with God should function.

All along, God had been trying to get me to shower my affections upon Him first, so that He could teach me how to love and submit to the husband He had already ordained for me. Suddenly, I felt spiritually retarded because it had taken me so long to finally understand what God was trying to do for me. Although I had repeatedly prayed for a husband, God had begun to answer that prayer by first teaching me how to be a wife, a Godly wife who loved and respected God as the head of her life.

Ephesians 5:22-24 likens a marriage relationship to that of the church, where God is clearly the head. A wife is expected to submit to her husband just as the church submits to Christ. These verses read, "Wives submit to your husbands as to the Lord. For the husband is the head of the wife as Christ is the head of the church, his body, of which he is the Savior. Now as the church submits to Christ, so also wives should submit to their husbands in everything."

Therefore, my husband will be a joy to serve and assist, because he clearly is required to exhibit Christ-like character in all his dealings. Christian women who married before allowing themselves to become spiritually enlightened must still respect their husbands as the head of the household even if they are not saved. Why? Because God has set a spiritual chain of command that governs spiritual and marriage relationships in I Corinthians 11:3, which reads, "But I want you to know that the head of every man is Christ, the head of woman is man, and the head of Christ is God."

Ultimately, everyone is subject to God, but women must respect man's place in God's divine order of things as spiritual leaders within the household. However, women are never, ever required to subject themselves to an abusive man. Remember that God did not create his word to be interpreted according to sexist or misogynistic ideologies, in order to oppress women. On the contrary, God is a God of order that governs the universe with spiritual laws that have been recorded for us in the Holy Scriptures, but most importantly, He himself is love and would never deal with His children in an unloving manner. Therefore, single women should cherish their privilege to correctly choose a mate according to God's spiritual criteria versus fleshly desires.

> *Dear God, thank you so much for revealing to me*
> *the characteristics of a Godly woman.*
> *I recognize that in my own strength I can never become*
> *a virtuous woman, but by your Holy Spirit, I can become*
> *the Godly woman and wife you desire for me to be.*
>
> *Release me from the fear of remaining unmarried*

and of incompatibility with the husband you have chosen for

me.

I want to always remember that you are a good God and
that you
give only good gifts to your children.

I acknowledge my desires to be married as a willingness
to receive this precious, spiritual gift that will not be
withheld,
but freely given to me by your hands in due and divine
time.

In Jesus' name I thank you that it is done.
Amen.

Chapter 5

✥

HUSBAND REVELATION

For your Maker is your husband,
The Lord of hosts is His name;
And your Redeemer is the Holy One of Israel;
He is called the God of the whole earth. (Isaiah 54:5)

After writing that marriage prayer, I soon realized that I had prayed for a husband, but not to become a wife. A male friend once asked me, "Are you prepared to support a man spiritually, physically and emotionally?" That question gave me pause for thought. "Was I?" I asked myself. Me, a woman who had declared that caring for a pet was too similar to caring for a child? In order to release my idyllic view of marriage and consider the realities of such a relationship, I began to think of some of my friends' marriages.

One friend had moved far from her family soon after marriage to pursue her husband's dreams of becoming a filmmaker. Because this field is exclusive and highly competitive, he did not work for a while, but eventually began to take odd jobs. My friend became the "breadwinner," and some of her professional plans had to be delayed when their first baby unexpectedly arrived right when their marriage had become strained.

Another friend married fresh out of college when she discovered that she was pregnant. Unfortunately, the baby was born prematurely and suffered with medical problems that required constant care. As a result, she worked only within the household and her social life consisted of caring for the baby and her husband. Although she has since had another child, the relationship with her husband is less than ideal. They are still together and love each other, but their firstborn put an unexpected strain on their marriage early on.

Reflecting upon the harsh realities of my friends' marriages made me stop asking God for a husband, because I was not sure I was prepared to be a wife and mother. Doing so made me realize that I had to get a clear understanding of the immense compromises and responsibilities a wife must undertake. In my reconsideration of marriage, I was also reminded that marriage could be a problem for Christians who married before coming into a true relationship with Christ, without asking for his guidance in selecting a partner.

Repentant believers can certainly pray and expect for God to heal their broken marriages, but God is not obligated to prosper anything that was done according to the flesh. Therefore, it is gravely important that single women avoid getting impatient by choosing to date or marry men that they have not consulted God about first. When in doubt about whether to become involved with a particular man, fasting will subdue the flesh long enough for you to hear clearly from God.

I further examined myself and found that I had not been entirely clear on what having a husband entailed. God knew this all the while I had been kicking, screaming and getting upset with Him over being unmarried. It is important to note that this kind of revelation comes directly from the Holy Spirit. No amount of watching Oprah or reading Iyanla Vanzant could have allowed me to assess myself this honestly without feeling condemned. John 16: 13 states that it is the Holy Spirit's job to lead us into all truth. "Howbeit when he, the Spirit of truth, is come, he will guide you into all truth…"(KJV). True spiritual enlightenment occurs when you ask the Holy Spirit to align your thoughts according to the wisdom and word of God.

REVELATION NUMBER TWO

One day after study and prayer, I realized that God had indeed been trying to honor my demand for a husband. He had been trying to teach me about love and faithfulness by drawing me into fellowship with Him first. How can a Christian woman love a Godly man before demonstrating true love for God?

In some areas of my life, I had been disobedient and unfaithful to God. This bitter truth was difficult, but necessary to acknowledge. I had not been paying tithes consistently. I had spent more time watching *Nickelodeon* than reading the Bible. My prayers were often brief and hurried as I dashed out the door in the morning, or drifted off to sleep at night. I attended church, but was often late. The Holy

Spirit revealed many personal things about my deficient relationship with Jesus. I learned that I could never have a successful relationship with a man, let alone be married, if I had not first established a solid relationship with Christ, my first husband. Romans 8:38-39 declares that nothing should interfere with our love relationship with Christ; not height, depth or any other created thing. "Created things" include attractive men we might want to date. I clearly understood that I certainly would not submit to a man prone to leave the toilet seat up, if I could not totally submit to God first.

UNDERSTANDING PRIORITIES

I stopped asking for a husband and set about giving God first priority in my life. God is a jealous God and will have no one, or no thing put before Him (Exodus 34: 14). God knew that if I had been given the man of my dreams before I practiced putting Him first, then I would have focused on pleasing the boyfriend, without seeking God as diligently as I have been. Loving God takes singleness of heart and requires that you involve your total being.

"Love the Lord your God with all your heart and with all your soul and with all your strength" (Deuteronomy 6:5 NIV).

When I realized that being single meant that I was free to love God fully without distraction, Jesus became my boyfriend. This freedom to worship God without the constraints of marriage and family is what Paul particularly enjoyed about the single life, and also admonished unmarried men and women to treasure as well. Paul was not discouraging anyone from marrying, but wanted men and women to put the marriage relationship in proper perspective. Married women in that culture and time had no legal rights to property or ownership of anything, because everything she had belonged to the husband. She was bound by law to regard her husband as her master, for as long as he lived, as Paul states in I Corinthians 7:39; however, single women were not.

Paul underscores the privilege of the single woman to minister to and for God in verse 34 of the same chapter. He writes, "The unmarried woman cares about the things of the Lord, that she may be holy both in body and in spirit." Now, this only applies to women who have crucified their flesh in order to pursue a life in the spirit, not those who still want to party and get their freak on!

Some of you might have <u>realized</u> these simple truths long ago, but unless they have caused you to change your life and priorities, then you have not been properly <u>convicted</u> of these truths. Conviction often comes through an old word given at the right season in our lives to free us from the strongholds that satan created in our minds to keep us estranged from God (John 8:31-32).

II Corinthians 5:17 says, "Therefore if any man be in Christ, he is a new creature: old things are passed away; behold, all things are become new" (KJV). Paul says that all that <u>be</u> in Christ, not simply have a knowledge of Him, are new creatures. In order to learn to abide in His love (I John 4:16) and <u>patiently</u> sit at his feet, old behaviors and thought patterns have to be pruned away.

REMOVING THE JUNK

Some people, friendships, as well as old desires that have hindered your relationship with God must pass from your life. It took a while for God to clear out old junk from my life, because I wanted to hang on to some of it! When I realized that I would never produce fruit the way God wanted me to if those things stayed, I began to loosen my grip bit by bit. When it seems that your friends are becoming fewer, that no men are calling you for dates and life as you once knew it is changing quickly, know that it is probably God working according to His word, rather than the devil trying to destroy you.

In John 15:2 Jesus states, "Every branch in Me that does not bear fruit He takes away; and every branch that bears fruit He prunes, that it may bear more fruit." In the previous verse, Jesus establishes that His father God does the pruning. In a botanical sense, pruning requires that weeds and other debris be uprooted, or forcibly removed from the thing that is trying to grow. In the third verse of this passage in John, Jesus says that we are clean through His word. Spiritually speaking, the word of God loosens and removes old thoughts, desires, behaviors and everything that is not conducive to our spiritual growth.

As A. W. Tozer so eloquently writes in *The Pursuit of God*, "To rip through the dear and tender stuff of which life is made can never be anything but deeply painful."[ii] Although this type of cleansing is very painful, we become free from the trappings of the world and liberated in Christ, if we endure the process.

RELEASING CONTROL

In the media and literature of all types, Black women have been portrayed as being strong, domineering and authoritative in a masculine sense. The residual effects of slavery have created the stereotype of Black women as being unfeminine workhorses, with bestial sexualities.

We see this concept played repeatedly in our everyday lives. In many social, work and family settings, Black women are often expected to carry the burden of responsibility for whatever tasks that need to be completed. However, Black women often treat themselves as pack mules by accepting an exorbitant amount of work. We can take it. Our female ancestors who endured much worse with far fewer resources survived and nurtured generations of progeny, so likewise, we as contemporary Black women should become superwomen without complaint or reservation.

This type of mentality has caused great emotional and physical distress within Black women. It is absolutely ridiculous to try to accommodate everyone in all things, but Black women often chastise themselves for being unable to successfully manage an excessive amount of responsibility. As a result, Black women are just as prone to cancer, heart disease and other stress related illnesses as white men reportedly are.

In church settings, Black women tend to participate in a variety of different ministries, or otherwise busy themselves with 'church work.' It is not unusual for a single woman to sing in the choir on first and third Sundays, serve as an usher on the second and fourth, attend single's meetings two Fridays out of the month, volunteer within the youth department, teach a Sunday School class, attend graduate school, maintain a full-time job, and chide herself for not having a separate social life.

Single women often over commit themselves in efforts to avoid feeling lonely, but the stress of trying to multitask too much at one time can lead to long-term health problems much worse than fleeting emotions like depression or loneliness. When people see Black women suffering from the mild and extreme effects of stress, like premature hair loss or disease, it is very difficult for them to see the radiance of a virtuous woman.

Is your worth really far above rubies when your otherwise beautiful face and attitude become drawn and unpleasant due to exhaustion? Society at large and Christians in particular, often mistrust and criticize a husband whose wife looks unkempt and unhealthy, because she reflects his success or failure as a good manager of his home. Very often, we choose elected officials, ministers and deacons based upon how attractive and robust their wife and children appear.

This type of subjective assessment of the husband and his family is confirmed in Proverbs 12:4 which reads, "An excellent wife is the crown of her husband, but she who causes shame is like a rottenness in his bones." Likewise, attractive, sexy, intelligent women represent Christ and the faith far better than women who neglect themselves physically, emotionally and spiritually because they are burdened with illness, or too much busy work.

THE TRUE MEANING OF SUBMISSION

In general, all women need to allow their husbands to fulfill their positions as heads of households by ceasing to vie for control that women were not originally intended to fight for. Black women in particular will have a more difficult time learning to release control to their husbands, because Black men have been depicted as incapable or unwilling to execute the role of husband as outlined in the scriptures.

On the other hand, I heard a popular television preacher proclaim to thousands of Black women that women who want to do everything themselves are stupid, because they were created to be provided for rather than be the providers. I had a problem with this opinion, because single women head over half of all Black families.

Therefore, Black women have been forced to take on more masculine responsibilities, because many men have eschewed their role as the head of the family. I listened a little further and received his point by revelation of the Holy Spirit.

Christian women need to understand that being a helpmate, or an assistant in the home does not mean that she is unequal or subservient to the man. In the Garden of Eden, Eve was not beaten or humiliated into serving God or Adam. She was not ridiculed for being more delicate or physically weaker. She was prized for those things and considered a beautiful partner to man. Although the first man and woman were given different types of work to do, the man was designed to carry the weight as the head, and the woman was created to help him bear that burden so that he would not die prematurely, or stress out in the process of being the spiritual and natural head of the family.

Single women need to realize that God is the husband and head of their households. Therefore, single women should cast their care upon the Lord (I Peter 5:7), because He really wants to care for them.

Single women often view themselves as being their own sole providers; however, if we say that God is first in our lives, then we need to demonstrate that by allowing Him to take care of our needs. Single women are in an excellent position to practice being a good wife with the most excellent husband of all, Christ.

Instead of fretting over financial problems, why not trust God to provide for that need? Instead of seeking comfort in possessions, sex or other people, why not trust God to heal you? Why carry the burden of providing for your own needs when the scriptures say that God will do that? Many single women have probably quoted Philippians 4:19 numerous times without fully understanding how that applies to their lives. This scripture in the New International Version of the Bible reads, "And my God will meet all your needs according to his glorious riches in Christ Jesus."

Does this scripture say that God will take care of your financial needs, but not the emotional ones? Does it say that God will pay your rent, but you are own your own with the electric, cable and grocery bill? We often limit God to caring for our physical or monetary needs when the Bible says He will take care of everything. Casting your care upon the Lord means to tell Him what all your concerns are and trust Him to resolve the problems in your life. How can we do this in a practical way? After you have committed your concerns to God, instead of seeking ways to fix the problem yourself, repeat every scripture you can recall about God providing for you, believing that He will not disappoint you by letting the problem remain.

True submission to God, or to a husband means having faith in their abilities to provide for your needs. Women demonstrate this best by refusing to fix what they have entrusted to the man. A good Godly woman will discover how to assist the man without overtaking him. An even better woman will edify God and the man by praising his efforts, blessing his path, and telling him how great and wonderful he is.

Why would a woman do these things for the man in her life? So that he can remain healthy and sound enough to keep providing for her! In fact, God and the man will be more apt to outdo themselves in granting her wants and desires when they receive this type of loving appreciation from her. Smart women will understand these concepts of releasing control and of submission, but wise women who embrace these spiritual truths will see the blessings attached to these principles manifest in their lives.

WHAT ARE HUSBANDS SUPPOSED TO DO?

In Matthew 19:4, Jesus tells the Pharisees that although Moses made provision for divorce within marriage, that God did not originally intend for marriages to be broken in this way. Likewise, God never intended for gender roles and the responsibilities of husbands and wives to become as perverted and misinterpreted as they have become. Women often hear a lot of balanced, as well as unbalanced teachings on the role of wives, but rarely are they taught what to expect from a Godly husband. If we look at how Adam, the first man, functioned in his relationships with God and Eve, as well as a few other scriptural qualities of a Christian husband, we can begin to get an understanding of God's original plan for the husband.

Ashan R. Hampton

All of the scripture for this section has been quoted from the New

Living Translation (NLT) of the Bible.

HUSBANDS ARE TO LIVE JOYFULLY WITH THEIR WIVES ALL THE DAYS OF THEIR LIVES.

Ecclesiastes 9:9: "Live happily with the woman you love through

all the meaningless days of life that God has given you in this world.

The wife God gives you is your reward for all your earthly toil."

Most of us have been persuaded to believe that the differences

between men and women will foster frequent arguments within a

marriage. However, this scripture suggests that when men view their

wives as a gift or reward from God that they can live peaceably with

her for as long as they live on this earth. A man who welcomes the

addition of a woman into his life, and treats her like a precious gift

from God, has a heart that is prepared to minister to his wife within a

marriage the way God intended.

HUSBANDS SHOULD BECOME ONE WITH THEIR WIVES.

Genesis 2:24: "This explains why a man leaves his father and mother and is joined to his wife, and the two are united into one." A husband should not have to move his family in with his parents! He is told to establish himself with his wife so that both of them can meld with one another spiritually and function as one body. This means that no other woman, relative or friend should be closer to a man than his wife, except God himself. Because the man is in spiritual sync with his wife and they are both being led by the Holy Spirit, he should not allow any external influences to disrupt his marital union, which has been ordained by God.

HUSBANDS SHOULD BE MONOGAMOUS.

Proverbs 5:15: "Drink water from your own well - share your love only with your wife." If a man sees nothing wrong with dating you while intermittently spending time with another woman, how ready is he to be committed to only one woman? Many westerners

are rapidly adopting religious marriage practices from other cultures

that allow multiple marriages. Many men of color from other

countries and traditions are converting to Christianity, but their

previous ideas about women and marriage are often slow to change.

Women assume that Christian men automatically practice

monogamy in their dating and marriage relationships, but

unfortunately, many do not. However, a mature Christian man

understands that God did not intend for him to scatter pieces of his

heart and body amongst several different women, but rather for his

total being to merge with only one woman in the most holy manner.

HUSBANDS SHOULD LEAD AND LOVE THEIR WIVES AS CHRIST LOVES THE CHURCH.

Ephesians 5:23, 25: "For a husband is the head of his wife as

Christ is the head of his body, the church; he gave his life to be her

Savior. And you husbands must love your wives with the same love

Christ showed the church (v. 25)." The only men who will be

potential marriage partners for you are those you respect as good leaders. Nothing is more frustrating than to dance with a man who is a weak lead, but a woman falls gracefully into the arms of a man who knows the steps and makes them easy for her to follow. A man should be prepared to love his woman as sacrificially as Christ loves His people. This man will not be selfish enough to withhold from his woman until she gives of herself first, but he will give of himself without expecting anything but her love in return.

HUSBANDS SHOULD NEVER BE ABUSIVE.

Colossians 3:19: "And you husbands must love your wives and never treat them harshly." Unfortunately, all of the physical, sexual, emotional and verbal abuse that occurs in the world against women is also experienced within Christian marriages. Women must understand that every man that professes Christianity has not allowed the power of the Holy Spirit to transform his lifestyle and thought life. We can only become Christ-like by the power and fruit of the Holy Spirit, but immature, carnal Christians often have not submitted themselves to the spiritual work that this entails. At first, a man's willingness to lead the relationship thrills a woman, but if the activity in the relationship becomes uncomfortably unequal, then the woman should look for the warning signs of potential abuse. In addition, if a man seems controlling, sarcastic, needy, or overly passive, pray for discernment and be ready to break with him if the Holy Spirit leads you to do so. Clearly, God intended for men to treat women gently with the love of Christ at all times.

HUSBANDS SHOULD MANAGE THE HOUSEHOLD.

I Timothy 3:4: "He must manage his own family well, with children who respect and obey him." As we have seen in previous scriptures, men should not rule his family with anger, abuse, or harsh language. Unfortunately, society has taught boys that being a man involves mild to extreme violence to control his environment. A Christian man realizes that he has been transformed by Christ's love, grace and mercy. Likewise, he should demonstrate these qualities in his relationships within and outside of his family. The management of a household consists of the proper stewardship of finances, food, shelter, emotions, etc. However, because one man cannot be expected to take all of this responsibility upon himself, it is the wife's duty to help the husband be successful in heading the family.

There are many other scriptures that delineate the characteristics of a Godly man, and I encourage all women to search them before getting involved with men who really are not prepared to be husbands. The stories of great men of the Bible like Boaz, in the Book of Ruth, and Hosea poignantly depict how Godly men show love and honor toward the women in their lives; whereas the Song of Solomon illustrates how sweetly a man and woman should revere one another in their hearts and in their speech.

It is important for single women to get a clear understanding of the realities of marriage. No marriage can be successful if the wife and husband are not clear about their particular roles and responsibilities. As you continue to ask God to show you His plan for marriage, you will realize just how sacred and precious it is compared to the world's false version of it.

Thank you Lord for revealing your true intentions for marriage to me.

Thank you Holy Spirit for showing me the areas of my heart and lifestyle that are not yet prepared for marriage.

I will honor my singleness as an opportunity to prepare to minister

to the wonderful man you have chosen for me, so that I will be a beautiful

and welcomed addition to his relationship with you, Heavenly Father.

Thank you that it is done.

Amen.

Chapter 6

❧

GOOD GIRLS DON'T

For the lips of an immoral woman drip honey,
And her mouth is smoother than oil;
But in the end she is bitter as wormwood,
Sharp as a two-edged sword.
Her feet go down to death,
Her steps lay hold of hell. (Proverbs 5:3-5)

Gifts are given, but fruit has to be developed. Before good growth can take place, the process of pruning has to be initiated. In fact, before seeds can be planted, the ground has to be prepared and cleared of any debris that might disrupt growth. I had entered the pruning process way before I realized what was going on, but I eventually thanked God for thinking enough of me to bring me to this point of consecration.

My phone did not ring sometimes for days at a time. God had spiritually sequestered me in order to bring me into a deeper level of fellowship with Him. Men did not ask me for dates, not because I was unattractive, but because God wanted me to acknowledge His love for me above anyone else's. I can't tell you how or when it happened, but suddenly life became more enjoyable despite my waning social life. Although I still struggled with finances and the single life, I began to praise God anyway. I even decided that I did not want a guy to interrupt the relationship Jesus and I had begun to develop.

Because I was no longer complaining about not having a man, conversations with some of my old girlfriends got short, or became sparse. Instead, I literally began admonishing my female friends to build a relationship with Jesus Christ, and to allow Him to prune their lives to reflect the holiness He as a holy God demands of His followers. I was amazed. A friend of mine even commented that I had gotten "all spiritual and stuff." Sometimes I felt like my old self was on the outside looking in awe at the new creature that God was fashioning.

The changes that had occurred in my attitude and perspective on life led me to further assess my lifestyle. Because of the spiritual overhaul the Holy Spirit had begun to work within me, I desired to live a totally clean life. Although I had not had sex in a long while, I never made a firm commitment to celibacy. Eventually, I had to have a completely honest and open discussion with God about my sexuality.

Many people who attend church have sex, but no one wants to talk about it. The increasing number of unwed teenage mothers wheeling their little ones down the aisles confirms this. We are quick to point fingers, transfer blame and preach that fornication is a sin, without equipping the members with the spiritual knowledge necessary to refrain from sexual sin.

I must admit that in the past I avoided scriptures in the Bible that refer to sex as a sin, because I could not make myself believe that it was all bad. For the record, God very much sanctions sex within the holy union of marriage. However, engaging in sexual activity outside of marriage only brings confusion, guilt and a whole host of negative consequences when what was to be a spiritual bond becomes carnal and must be broken.

Whenever you have sex with someone, married or not, you create a spiritual bond with that person. Why else have we gotten crazy when the guy began to see someone else, or refused to return our phone calls? Have you ever noticed how many stupid things you did or allowed to be done to you, because you just could not seem to let that guy go? God really wanted to protect us from all that drama by commanding that the act be reserved for the sanctity of marriage.

Satan has corrupted God's holy intentions for sex by obscuring its sacredness and the extreme consequences of fornication. Some people are silly enough to believe that they can deal with pregnancy, disease, or a tarnished reputation, but many do not contemplate the lacerations to the soul that fornication inflicts. I Corinthians 6:16 (KJV) chastises, "What? Know ye not that he which is joined to an harlot is one body? For two, saith he, shall be one flesh."

The sexual union between a man and woman represents the joining of their bodies and spirits that this verse speaks of. Just as bodily fluids are exchanged during sexual contact, so are spirits. Satanic rituals always involve a sex act, because that is how the satanists transfer demon spirits among each other. Therefore, when you have sex with multiple men, you also absorb the nature of their spirit.

God said that a man marries to leave his father and mother to cleave to his wife with whom he will become one flesh in Ephesians 5:32. When you surrender yourself physically and spiritually to an honest, sanctified, Godly man in a marriage, then you also benefit from the fruit and Godly character that God has formed in his spirit. Likewise, as unmarried women, when we invite Jesus Christ into our lives, He sends His Holy Spirit to abide within us. As a result, we are bound to a loving relationship with Christ.

There are many scriptures in which God has likened Himself and His relationship with us as a groom to a bride, so that we can realize the magnitude of our commitment to Him. Therefore, when women have sex with guys who seem really fine at the moment, they have just broken their sacred commitment to God as His bride. No woman wants to think of herself as being a harlot, but what do you call a woman who constantly cheats on her benevolent, faithful husband with immoral men? Fortunately, Jesus will cleanse our hearts and redeem our souls from sexual immorality. This type of redemption is most poignantly depicted in the Book of Hosea. God commanded the prophet Hosea to take the prostitute Gomer as his wife to demonstrate the unconditional love God demonstrates toward His chosen, though wayward, people.

Before I understood the consequences of fornication, I ran into a 'radical' female who had been celibate for three years. After hearing her testimony, I literally prayed that I would not have to wait that long. However, Romans 8:8 (KJV), "So then they that are in the flesh cannot please God," very clearly tells us that we have a choice where this area of our lives is concerned; to please God or not.

Granted, old habits are hard to break and the flesh does not die easily. People must deal with the issue of sex as God convicts them, but the Bible is very clear about the consequences of sexual sin. These mandates are there to help us guard our hearts against sin, not to condemn us for desiring to have sex. God intended for us to glorify Him with our sexuality; hence, Adam and Eve were to be "fruitful and multiply." Before Adam and Eve, the first married couple, fell into sin, they were both naked and were not ashamed (Genesis 2:25). When God pronounced them man and wife, they consummated their relationship before Him with no guilt or condemnation. Therefore, God created sex and He made it good!

A male friend told me that he dated a girl in his church who proclaimed that she would not hug or hold hands with a guy until she was married. I told him that this was unhealthy, not holiness. Another male friend reminded me that we all have different points of limitation so that what might seem to be harmless hand holding could in fact be a point of temptation for others. As Christians, we should pray to have a balanced, Christ-centered perspective on sex and affection, versus religious ideologies that are rooted in fear and condemnation.

Although many understand these truths about sex, honestly, many of us are celibate for a lack of opportunity. However, when you sincerely desire to crucify your flesh of sexual lust, you can only maintain freedom and deliverance through fierce obedience to God's word. The scripture debunks that carnal 'we all sin and fall short of the glory' argument that many worldly Christians use to excuse their prurient behavior. Activating God's grace in our lives does not exempt us from being punished for our sins. Hebrews 10:26 says, "For if we sin willfully after that we have received the knowledge of the truth, there remaineth no more sacrifice for sins."

THE BATTLE FOR SEXUAL PURITY

The enemy, however, will not allow you to refrain from sex without a fight. There are never any good rationalizations for sin, but when faced with the idea of relinquishing the tactile sensations of sex, we have all been guilty of listening to lies. Sometimes as a result of your fleshly desires, or conversations with other fornicators, you might entertain thoughts like, *"If you don't, then you won't be youthfully attractive, or the older you get the more likely you will have 'woman problems' if you don't."* I actually had a white male doctor tell me that I would have to get pregnant or take pain killers to abate my reproductive problems, which to a distorted, carnal ear sounded like he was suggesting that I have more sex.

However, right when I desired to unofficially commit myself to celibacy, media reports on the benefits of sexual activity seemed to come out of nowhere. *Women's skin appears more clear and supple afterward. A woman's physical body becomes firm and more attractive; her self-esteem increases, etc., etc.* I had already determined these and other benefits to sexual activity before hearing the reports, and unfortunately, my carnal nature had found most of these observations to be accurate. However, for unmarried believers, having sex will only reap corruption to their physical bodies and souls. Galatians 5:16 very simply conveys the solution to such fleshly struggles. "Walk in the Spirit, and you shall not fulfill the lust of the flesh."

It is not always easy to live a totally consecrated life while single, especially when so many Christians seem not to be living in holiness. Other people I know have dates all the time while I spend most of my weekends studying and writing. Some have tons of friends while my social circle has grown increasingly smaller. Some still have sex and have a good time doing it, but I cannot. As I Peter 2:9 says, followers of Christ are a strange and peculiar people, not just to sinners, but also to carnal Christians, or those Christians who have not completely separated from worldly pleasures. In this walk with Christ, peer pressure cannot excuse the occasional 'sin breaks' that some revert to when it seems that the standards of a holy lifestyle are unattainable based upon the behavior of other Christians who seem to prosper despite their sinful lifestyles. These types of observations often fuel discussions about holiness and the single Christian that are common to all single's ministries, regardless of denomination or geographic location.

I was in a single's meeting once where a young lady shared her concerns about what she had been told about attracting like spirits, and the fact that she had been meeting men who eventually propositioned her for sex. She said that men would politely shake her hand, ask if she were married, but soon after, their conversation turned into a lustful appraisal of her physical attractiveness.

I knew the look of lust she mentioned well. This look is really similar to that glazed over look a puppy gets when his tummy is rubbed in just the right spot. As she recounted her experiences, I was reminded of when I first moved to Atlanta and dealt with carnal men I met in nightclubs who had approached me in a similar fashion. It dawned on me that for a short while even after I stopped going to clubs that men on the street would hoot at me, or get that little lusty look whenever they spoke to me; be it at the grocery store, the gas station, or places where that type behavior was generally the least expected.

I usually did not speak in these type meetings, but before I knew it I blurted out, "You know that same thing happened to me." I was surprised to know that someone else had also had such a similar experience to mine. I remember exactly what I said to the young lady, because it was a supreme exercise in tact for me. I said, "I don't know how clear you are on that issue, but when I got clear about it, people stopped approaching me in that way." That was my euphemistic way of saying that men can sense when a woman wants to have sex, just as males within the animal kingdom know when a female is in heat.

Some men are more sophisticated than others when approaching sexually available women, but men's sexual instincts drive their pursuit of women despite how charming or 'saved' they appear to be. Basically, in both of our situations, the lust that resided in that girl, and me, had stirred up the lust in those men. The length of time we had refrained from sex before meeting those men was not the issue. The truth is that we had not closed the door to fornication, and as a result, sexual lust remained alive in our flesh.

I didn't tell her that it seemed like I could not pay a man to speak to me after I made some decisions about my sex life, partly because that was not true. I still caught the attention of men, which helped to keep my self-esteem intact, but I no longer had to deal with an excessive amount of unwanted advances. The young lady did not respond to what I said, but I got the feeling she understood exactly

what I did not say while in the company of others.

CONSEQUENCES OF SEXUAL SIN

Sex is still satan's favorite mode of temptation and attack.

Unfortunately, there are far too many women and young girls who

have been adversely affected by either consensual or nonconsensual

sexual activity.

I have a good college friend who accidentally got pregnant at a

time when she had just decided to begin a new relationship with a

male friend of hers. For a few months, she battled with

disappointment in herself for allowing it to happen, the decision to

keep the child, and how her friends and family would perceive her as

a single parent.

If she had not already had a spiritual foundation to return to, this

situation would have been a prime opportunity for satan to destroy

her emotionally and physically if she had decided to have an

abortion. This type of trauma is not what God intended for us, but because we as humans possess free will, we have the ability to choose to enter into sin, or to flee from it.

The choices are really very simple: Keep doing it and suffer the consequences, or stop and live within the will of God. Once again the word very clearly tells us what the consequence will be if we continue to take 'sin breaks,' or to maintain fleshly vices, which the world says are acceptable to have. Therefore, many single Christians see nothing wrong with frequenting 'Christian' clubs, having sex, drinking, smoking, wearing provocative clothing (to church), getting tattoos, body piercings, cursing, etc., etc. Many scriptures state that life in the flesh will lead to death. "For if ye live after the flesh, ye shall die: but if ye through the Spirit do mortify the deeds of the body, ye shall live" (Romans 8:13 KJV).

For women, especially young women, the issue of sex is replete with double standards, because we are the inheritors of the free sex and women's rights movements of the 60's and 70's. As a result, women in the 21st century feel freer to express themselves sexually and to acquire more partners. The rationale for this behavior is of the "we can do whatever men do" mentality, which means that since men have had numerous sexual partners and extramarital affairs, that women should exert their power to do the same. Hence, teen pregnancy is at an incredibly high rate, as is abortion, and so are instances of cervical cancer in young women under thirty. There are practical and spiritual reasons to abstain, but most of us are more familiar with and even intrigued by the sociocultural one.

GOOD GIRLS DON'T

Young men are taught that sex is a natural part of manhood, whereas young girls are taught that only 'bad girls' engage in pre-marital sex. Therefore, when men decide to settle down and look for a 'good girl,' they look for virgins, or in this day and age, a girl with little sexual experience. However, given the tolerance to sin we experience in our current society and in our churches, finding a male or female over twenty who has remained a virgin is possible, but for the most part unlikely.

Many young men, especially within the Christian community, believe in this 'good girl' ideal. They might openly share their past sexual experiences with you, but do you honestly think they can handle hearing about yours? Remember the guy friend I thought for sure was my soul mate? We broached this issue when he told me that he had fornicated with a girl he only superficially liked just two weeks before our conversation. I mentioned that I had been celibate for a long while. He immediately wanted to know the exact length of time.

I asked why it mattered, since he obviously had not been celibate. He responded by admitting that he was a male chauvinist pig, and did not want to get serious about a girl who was sexually active. He was only twenty-five years old, but still clung to this ancient socialized idea of the 'good girl.' Do you think that the single men who attend church have totally committed to a life of sexual purity? Maybe a few of them have, but almost all of them will expect the woman they get serious about to have done so, and if you want to be that woman, then celibacy is expected of you. Most importantly, God expects you to keep your body holy.

In I Corinthians 6:18-20, Paul admonishes believers to "flee fornication," and reminds us that our bodies are not our own, but have been bought with a price. Verse 18 in the New Living Translation of the Bible reads, "Run away from sexual sin! No other sin so clearly affects the body as this one does. For sexual immorality is a sin against your own body." (So is prostitution.) Notice that Paul was never married, but he frequently counseled the Corinthians and Thessalonians, in particular, on matters of sex and marriage. He was able to do so because the source of their struggles stemmed from the opposition between fleshly desires and spiritual laws. Believers through the centuries have long been vexed about the issue of fornication, a fact that once consoled me, because I was obviously not alone in my struggles.

I had a very honest conversation with God about this issue, and as a result, He did me a huge favor. He arranged it so that I did not have the opportunity to be tempted in this way, unless I initiated it, which I did not. This is the enlightened view of my long running dating dry spell! Because I think this will bless others, I will share with you how I came to the point of celibacy.

Quite simply, all of a sudden, I could not do it. I tried, but I just could not go through with the act. Prior to that, however, I literally felt filthy for days after having sex. This was a new experience for me, because in my worldly Christian days, I felt quite relaxed afterward, but when I began to feel like I had actually sinned, I knew it was time to just quit. I don't know about you, but I need a lot of blessings from God to befall me in a short amount of time, so I decided to stop blocking them by living in disobedience to God.

SUBDUING THE FLESH

When I became aware that I had entered the sanctification process, I distinctly recall asking myself inwardly "That too?" The answer for me was, "Yes, that too!" Every woman must find her own answers in this life, but the Bible specifically says not to fornicate.

The word fornication, as used in the scriptures, does refer to illicit sexual intercourse. Interestingly enough, a popular book that has just recently been released, discussing sex and spirituality, argues that the word "fornication" originally meant to have sex with prostitutes. In the book *Oh God! A Black Woman's Guide to Sex and Spirituality*, Rev. Dr. Susan Newman argues that women who engage in pre-marital sex and masturbation should not feel guilty for doing so, because the cultural laws that forbid these things only apply to the ancient Hebrews, and not us 21st century, American gentiles. Therefore all the scriptures that admonish us to flee fornication only apply to patrons of prostitutes. This is an excellent example of the type of deception and false teachings that are paving the way for a more intense manifestation of the spirit of anti-Christ, which is now already among us. (**Side note**: Beware of 'spiritual' leaders with too many titles before their names. **Second side note**: The author admitted that she chose the title to connote despair and sexual climax, so is this a source you can trust for spiritual truth?)

For the record, according to the *Strong's Exhaustive Concordance of the Bible*, "fornication" is derived from the Hebrew word "porneia," which refers to illicit sexual intercourse, adultery, homosexuality, lesbianism, intercourse with animals, sex with close relatives, sex with a divorced man or woman, and also metaphorically refers to the worship of idols.

Interestingly enough, Bishop Eddie Long of the New Birth Missionary Baptist Church in Atlanta, Georgia provocatively demonstrates how we all participate in prostitution in seemingly harmless ways. In his tape series, "Let's Talk About Sex," Bishop Long asserts that every time we pay for a movie with heavy sexual content, or cable movie channels, that we are in a sense participating in prostitution, because we are giving money to a source that provides sexual pleasure and titillation. What a valid and thought provoking point. And we wonder why we, the church, cannot operate in spiritual, Holy Ghost power? Paul warned us that in the last days, people would adopt doctrines specifically designed for their "itching ears."

For the time will come when they will not endure

sound doctrine; but after their own lusts shall they

heap to themselves teachers, having itching ears;

And they shall turn away their ears from the truth,

and shall be turned unto fables. (II Timothy 4: 3-4 KJV)

Instead of adhering to the holiness of God, and His commands to live in the world, but not according to the world, false teachers who profess Christ, are developing messages that encourage people to live according to their lusts and selfish desires, because the ways of God are too difficult to adhere to in this day and time. However, although some cling to the eternal salvation, "once saved-always saved" argument, Jesus himself said that not everyone who calls upon him will enter into heaven.

Not everyone that saith unto me, Lord, Lord, shall

enter into the kingdom of heaven; but he that doeth

the will of my Father which is in heaven.

Many will say to me in that day, Lord, Lord, have we

not prophesied in thy name? And in thy name have

cast out devils? And in thy name done many

wonderful works?

And then will I profess unto them, I never knew you:

depart from me, ye that work iniquity. (Matthew 7: 21-

23 KJV)

According to these words that Jesus spoke, there will be some

ministers and other church-going Christians who will be deceived

into thinking that they are ministering from the spirit of God, when

in fact they have been working against Him. Consider this. Can you

still continue to have sex, knowing how God feels about it, die

tomorrow and get in heaven? None of us can judge the things of

God, but are you willing to take a chance on your <u>own</u>

interpretations of God's love, forgiveness and judgment? Can you

see how important it is to have your own personal relationship and

surety with God, instead of debating crazy questions and doctrinal

issues like this?

Now that you no longer have to ponder God's stance on the issue of sex, you must decide whether or not you want to live according to God's good pleasure for your life, and refrain from sexual relationships, or live in rebellion to God's word concerning this matter. I have chosen to do God's will, and to live as best as I can according to kingdom principles so that I can receive kingdom benefits.

Unfortunately, some of you, or others you know, have entered into unlawful relationships convinced that God will bless it to flourish into a committed marriage relationship. It seems to have worked for some people, but very often, down the road, those relationships end in divorce, or are otherwise severed. Hopefully with the information you have now obtained about the single life and your walk with Jesus Christ, you can avoid the temptation to become sexually active, or otherwise "unequally yoked" with carnal Christians or unbelievers.

REVELATIONS ABOUT MASTURBATION

This is a brand new section that was not previously included in any of the previous thirteen drafts of this manuscript that I have laboriously edited and revised, because it is a touchy, taboo subject that I was not going to attempt to address for these reasons. The Holy Spirit, however, has given me some interesting insights into this subject that I feel compelled to share with you.

❧

As alternatives to sex, particularly partner sex, the media, Jocelyn Elders, the church, and a whole host of individuals and organizations in our society, promote masturbation as a "safe sex" alternative to sexual intercourse. Their arguments can be quite persuasive. Oh, they say that self-touch helps adolescents, late bloomers and non-orgasmic women to learn more about their bodies and what feels good to them, which will eventually enable them to communicate all this to a partner, who will then join them in achieving complete sexual satisfaction. You can't get pregnant, or contract sexually transmitted diseases by stimulating yourself, and on and on the benefits continue.

Teenagers and single women seem to be the targets of all these discussions on masturbation. Why? Because if women of all ages pleasured themselves, as opposed to having sex with a man, then the birth rate could be controlled a little better, without having to adopt governmental rules that limit the number of children a couple or individual can have, like some Asian countries do.

However, single American women are expected to masturbate, because it is assumed that they will have fewer partners available to them than men. On the other hand, men are encouraged to have sex with as many women as possible, while women are encouraged to buy inanimate gadgets to simulate sexual pleasure. In churches, women are told that Godly men will want to marry a celibate woman, but men are allowed to have sex with any willing woman, in or outside of the church, until they finally get married, because men need sex to live, and women want it for no other reason than just to have it.

Anyway, the media is encouraging single women to masturbate in response to the universal man shortage that is precluding them from receiving a steady dose of sexual pleasure from a waning pool of available male partners. For example, on a recent *Ricki Lake* show, several women of different races wanted help in finding a potential mate. So, the show employed a variety of methods to assist these women in their search, such as online matchmaking services, speed dating and blind dating. They also included a segment on sex toys for those in between times when Mr. Right is nowhere in sight. However, another show called *Berman and Berman*, hosted by two sisters who are doctors, hosted an entire segment talking about masturbation and other aspects of female sexuality later that night. They also demonstrated a variety of dildos that stimulate different areas of the female genitalia.

If the mere mention of sex toys is making you blush, then this next little anecdote will really blow your mind. In college, a group of students I traveled with to Spain decided to experience a bona fide,

European sex shop. I saw one object that looked like a penis, and my

eyes just became blinded with embarrassment, so that I really could

not see anything else. (Or was that the Holy Spirit shielding me?)

Well, a few years later, once I became a grown up, a colleague and I

on a trip to New York, as a joke, decided to enter an adult sex shop,

since it was right there on the corner. This time I saw some of the

stuff that was in there. Skimpy, multi-colored pieces of cloth hung

from the ceiling. I couldn't tell which pieces you wore, and which

covered your eyes. Then a very anxious male sales clerk ushered us

over to the dildo counter.

I was astonished by the many varieties, colors, styles and sizes

there were. My colleague and I tried to politely move on out of the

store, until he showed us one that stuck to the wall; one that twirled

around with little blinking lights; some rainbow colored 'massagers,'

and the more flesh toned ones that were made of material to simulate

human flesh. The sizes ranged from enormous to small, depending

on the talents of the woman buying it. Don't try to front like this is all new territory for you, super spiritual Christian woman, because some of you have something in your underwear drawers right now that requires batteries, water, or some other form of lubrication. If He hasn't already, the Holy Spirit will badger you, until you get rid of all that stuff like He did me! The point of my story was to show you the extent to which we have all been influenced by unGodly advice from the media, with regard to female sexuality. Many of you might have begun this practice as an innocent means of stress release, or to please your freaky boyfriend. Some of you might be convinced that masturbation is a harmless, necessary part of your Christian lifestyle.

What is wrong with masturbation? It keeps you in bondage that later manifests into an unhealthy addiction. Because God loves us, he wants us to be free from wordly, satanic influence in every area of our lives, so the following revelations are given out of the spirit of love, not condemnation.

THE TRUTH ABOUT MASTURBATION

Masturbation opens the door to the flesh and serves as a gateway for demonic activity. When the flesh is aroused, it precludes spiritual activity. Romans 8:5,8 very clearly states that fleshly activity does not please God, because it separates us from communion with Him in the spirit. How so? Because our minds become focused on self and satisfying the flesh as opposed to the things of God. The following verses demonstrate this concept more clearly:

> For they that are after the flesh do mind the things of
> the flesh; but they that are after the Spirit the things of
> the Spirit.
>
> So then they that are in the flesh cannot please God.
> (Romans 8:5,8)

Therefore, masturbation is an unacceptable practice for the Christian woman, because it caters to the satisfaction of the flesh, and is not pleasing to God.

Teasing and titillating your flesh in this way creates a hunger for heightened or more intense stimulation and pleasure. You might practice masturbation thinking that it is simply your stress buster that you look forward to at night after a hard day at the office, but eventually, with continued practice, you will become addicted. Before you know it, your flesh will not only cry out for pleasure at night during your 'quiet moments' when no one can see you, but during the day, as well, when you are trying to concentrate on job tasks. Just like a smoker who will brave the rain, wind and snow for a few puffs in the designated smoking section outside the building, you too will have to fight the strength of your addiction on a minute-by-minute basis.

The more you feed your flesh the stronger and hungrier it gets. Eventually, your flesh will tell you that it needs a more intense form of stimulation than your hands or toys can provide; now enters pornography, sexual fantasies, day dreaming, and a general obsession with sexual pleasure. Note that the first of the nine satanic statements in the satanic Bible deals with the pleasure of the flesh:

"Satan represents indulgence instead of abstinence." Because the flesh can never be satisfied, it propels you to do whatever it takes to get the next rush of pleasure, no matter how brief or dangerous it is. According to the satanic principle above, such bondage to the flesh is satanically designed.

Now, as with any addiction, you are bound to your flesh and separated from God, because He is a spirit and you are now minding the things of the flesh, which do not please God. Your soul is out of alignment with your spirit, because it is operating independently of the Holy Spirit to fulfill its own lusts, according to satan's influence and temptations. Just as marijuana is called a gateway drug into harder drugs, despite claims of its milder effects, masturbation can be a gateway to sexual perversions such as lesbianism, group sex, domination, or exhibitionism. Satan might also use this toehold to create various other strongholds in your mind, because he doesn't play fair. Once you have opened yourself up to demonic influence in any form, he has a right to oppress you in any way he chooses.

DELIVERANCE FROM SEXUAL LUST

If you feel that you have a problem with sexual issues, then know that this realization is from the Holy Spirit who wants to heal you by loving the wounds away, not by condemning you. Your deliverance can begin right now just by having a completely honest conversation with God. Bare your soul and tell Him all that you have done, thought and felt about your body and sexual relationships. Although God knows everything about you, exposing your heart with your own mouth will destroy satan's ability to accuse you and make you feel guilty about what you have done in darkness (i.e. spiritual ignorance and immaturity).

Just remember that God's light of truth will free you, where as satan's tricks to make you feel foolish by talking to God in this way will keep you bound. When a mob of men brought the woman who had been caught in the very act of adultery before Jesus for judgment, He pardoned her transgressions, rather than condemn her for them. Jesus made her accusers disappear, and told her to go and sin no more. (See John 8: 1-12). Do you think this woman continued to commit adultery after this encounter with Jesus? Although it is not recorded, I don't think she did, because Jesus, with His loving words and actions, healed the <u>root</u> of her pain, so that she would not have to commit this sin anymore.

Know that addiction or unGodly behavior is simply the manifestation of a deep hurt that might not have anything to do with sex, or the problem that appears on the surface. The Holy Spirit deals with the heart, or the core of your very being; with the deep things of God, not human superficialities.

"A righteous man may have many troubles, but the Lord delivers him from them all" (Psalm 34:19 NIV). Meditate on this and other deliverance scriptures, and deliverance from sexual immorality will be yours. It might not come instantaneously, and you might not <u>feel</u> any different right away, but in time, you will begin to notice changes in your thoughts and behaviors, if you allow the Holy Spirit to begin his healing and purging work within you.

Dear Holy Spirit,

Help me to understand God's will for my sex life and sexual desires.

I have not always considered God's feelings about my sexual expression, but I sincerely want to align my lifestyle with the word of God.

Please help me to do that.

I admit right now that giving up this sinful act that has brought me pleasure in the past will be extremely difficult for me emotionally and psychologically, but I am committed to releasing everything in my life that is not pleasing to God.

I want to stand within the grace and holy presence of God without any hidden sin, guilt, shame or hypocrisy.

I truly want my life to reflect the obedience and love I have for Christ.

Thank you that it is done.

Amen.

Chapter 7

๑๑

UNEQUALLY YOKED

*Do not be unequally yoked together with unbelievers.
For what fellowship has righteousness with
lawlessness?
And what communion has light with darkness? (II
Corinthians 6:14)*

Many of us know males and females alike who seem to have

fallen by the wayside, who could no longer deal with the loneliness

and emptiness the single life can bring. As a result, they have entered

physical relationships with people who have not completely

separated from carnality. Although women voice their frustrations

about the single life more so than men, there are actually many

young men who have a strong desire to be married, but who also

want God to express the perfect woman for them, straight from

heaven, all wrapped in heavenly glory, with a big silvery neon sign that blinks, "I'm the one!" Oh, we all have wished that it would happen like that; then we could easily avoid making wrong choices when seeking a mate.

One male friend shared with me that he was in fact getting to the point where raising his own family and finding the right person to marry were important goals for him, but he felt he needed to work and become wealthy first to provide his family with all the material items his parents had given him. So work became his focus, as it does for many singles. Businesses of all types truly love to hire single people who have nothing else to do but work at all hours of the day and night for less money, and promises of promotion!

However, since I began writing this book, this same friend quickly married a girl that none of our mutual friends knew. He contacted me after a two-year break in our friendship soon after he married. He was absolutely miserable. He knew that she was not the girl he wanted to marry, but she threatened to have an abortion if he did not propose to her. His father, who had recently entered the seminary, convinced him that marrying this girl and caring for the child was the 'spiritually correct' thing to do. I told him that God could turn this situation for the better, upon his repentance, but that the pain of fornication and making wrong choices would have to precede the healing. Incidentally, this was the same guy I swore was my soul mate.

Another male friend, who had been promoted fairly well at his job, once said, "Yeah, I'm getting tired of meeting all these country girls who think they are something and have nothing to offer." Although he desired to meet a woman of substance, he continued to frequent bars and clubs after work where drunken women propositioned him for sex. He secretly hoped that Miss Right would happen into one of those places for him to meet, marry and live happily ever after with.

As single people, we have all had similar thoughts of continuing to adopt the world's way of finding a mate. Honestly, sometimes waiting on God in this area can be difficult and depressing, especially when you awake at two in the morning to realize that only you and a pile of pillows are there listening to the darkness.

Sometimes you feel as if God has forgotten your desire to marry. At one point, I just pled with God to allow me to meet a nice man, period, and then we could negotiate the marriage part later.

Sometimes in the heat of battling with these fears and doubts, some of us succumb to them by returning, even if momentarily, to old worldly behaviors, not because we do not love God, but because we fear He has forgotten this petition we have asked of Him. We do not mean to intentionally disobey God, but for a moment, we get tired of hoping and living in faith on this issue. Unfortunately, these 'fainting' moments represent the most opportune time for satan to make us act according to fear, which is the antithesis of faith. Remember that satan came to tempt Jesus in the wilderness after forty days, when He was tired, not after the fifth day, when Jesus would have been brimming with vim and vigor.

My mother once told me that it seemed I always wanted to quit something just when I had already gotten to the end. Galatians 6:9 (KJV) admonishes us to "not be weary in well doing: for in due season we shall reap, if we faint not." Many of us run out of steam right when we are almost about to break through to our blessings. It is during these lapses of faith and energy that many have become unequally yoked.

II Corinthians 6:14 (KJV) "Be ye not unequally yoked together with unbelievers; for what fellowship hath righteousness with unrighteousness? And what communion hath light with darkness?" has been recited to unmarried people everywhere so often, and for so long that if a dime would have been set aside for all those times, the national deficit would no longer be an issue. Sometimes it seems that unequally yoked couples are in love and prosperous. We have all seen them. They drive fancy cars, have cute kids, and take long vacations, but as Christians, we do not envy the prosperity of the wicked. (We just cut our eyes at it, and ask God when He plans to bless us likewise.) However, many people are suffering in these type relationships, whether they are aware of it or not.

UNDERSTANDING "UNEQUALLY YOKED"

So what does being unequally yoked mean exactly? Is this phrase simply making a distinction between Christians and non-Christians? I submit to you that it also refers to unlike thoughts and different levels of spiritual development; therefore, relationships between two Christians can still be unequally yoked. Let me give a few examples of how we see this 'unequally yoked' phenomenon at work in our everyday lives.

I would talk to a particular girl friend frequently about men. We often swapped dating horror stories and encouraged one another to expand our educational and social interests. One day I called her, after several months of not hearing from her, and she said, "You know I'm pregnant right?" As she told the particulars, my heart dropped, because I felt I had lost my partner in this battle to live the single life successfully. The guy was nine years younger, living with his mother and was between jobs. In contrast, she was a professional young woman, who decided to have a good time dating this guy while still searching for Mr. Right.

She was convinced that their relationship would work, that the baby would be raised properly, and they would eventually be married; once he came of age. Did I mention they were living together while working to make all these things come to pass? The last time I talked with her, she angrily whispered to me how sick and tired she was of her boyfriend playing Nintendo with a group of friends whenever she came in from work. He was only 19 years old and she was 28. What did she expect from a child?

Another friend of mine. Another attractive young lady who also had given up on ever finding a decent man in Atlanta. She had dated and lived in Atlanta for six years and was all set to leave, until she went to a club one night to meet up with some friends, and met a man who became her boyfriend. He took good care of her; his parents liked her and life was wonderful now that she had a man. Sure, he was divorced, and struggled with his ex-wife to maintain some semblance of a relationship with his children. However, he was gainfully employed and did whatever she asked him to.

She called me one day after a few months of not having talked, when her boyfriend was out of town. I had no plans on that beautiful Saturday afternoon and she said, "Oh, now I know how you must feel." That attempt at friendly commiseration, translated in the language of the single meant, "Oh, how pathetic and lonely you must feel on a daily basis with no man to enjoy time with." After two years of dating this 'wonderful' man, she decided that his kids were bad and he would never be financially able to support the lavish lifestyle she dreamed of. She took a higher paying job in another city, but still communicated with him, until she began to date someone else.

Another friend of mine has been married for about four years, has a new baby, but her husband is not a Christian. She knew when she married him that he professed to be a pseudo-atheist, but now she feels a desire to align herself according to God's word, the way she had been trained as a child to do, but what will become of the marriage if she grows more attached to God, and her husband refuses to be saved? On one occasion, she called to tell me how excited she was about the church she had joined, and her hopes that her husband would eventually join as well. Several months later, however, her excitement was replaced with a litany of excuses as to why she could no longer attend.

During one of those moments when I thought God just wanted me to be lonely, I tried to spend time with a nice, funny guy who drank, smoked and performed comedy sets in nightclubs. That lasted about a month before I became intolerant of his worldly ways and foul, though comedic, communications. Shortly afterward, I met an attractive Christian guy, who talked the spiritual talk, but for some reason, after our first conversation, I did not feel that I could even be his friend.

At first I thought I was being overly picky, or that I had been alone for so long that I had forgotten how to relate to a man, but I soon discovered that sex was still an option for him. I finally cut off all conversation when he told me, jokingly of course, how much he would like to make wild, passionate love to me. This is <u>exactly</u> why

Christianity suffers much ridicule and offense, because sinners often meet 'church folk' before they find someone who has genuinely adopted a Godly lifestyle.

You know, as well as I, other Christians who have children out of wedlock, or have packed up to follow a partner across several states to live with them, but not marry them. There are unmarried and divorced pastors in churches worldwide, who are dating unsaved men and women, or babes in Christ. There are Christian men and women waiting for their 'soul mates' to leave their spouses for them, who warm your pews every Wednesday night and Sunday morning. Many divorces occur between couples that suddenly find they have nothing in common, or no longer want to deal with their partner's shortcomings. So this issue of being "unequally yoked" not only plagues single Christians, but people in general who are in relationships; however, 'church folk' in particular need to understand what being unequally yoked means in order to avoid linking themselves to people who have not been convicted to live a Godly lifestyle.

INVOKING DIVINE DETERMINATION

We must move beyond professing belief in God to living according to God's will. Matthew 7:13-14 tells us that wide is the gate, and broad is the way that leads to destruction, but strait is the gate, and narrow is the way that leads to life. If it were easy to live for God, then everyone would do it. As unmarried Christians, we struggle daily with the fact that our current world does not encourage righteous living, which constantly places us in a position to choose life and God, every waking second, and even in our dreams.

I am writing to encourage myself first then others to not lose all you have gained with God while waiting on Him to move in this area of your life. Mark 11:22 tells us to have faith in God. Demonstrate your faith by not moving ahead of God to obtain your own mate. Instead, concentrate on successfully completing the tasks God has created for you in your daily life. Pray that the Holy Spirit will guide your steps toward the mate He has chosen for you, instead of devising your own schemes to meet someone.

When Abraham sent his trusted servant to get a wife for Isaac, the servant prayed that God would reveal the right girl by a sign. When Rebekah was chosen, she was performing her daily tasks of watering the camels. Isaac was meditating in a field when he was introduced to his beautiful new wife. This entire account is recorded in Genesis 24. Singles can learn a couple of good life lessons from Isaac and Rebekah's story. First, we should faithfully carry out our daily responsibilities while waiting to meet our mates. Secondly, when we allow God to order our steps toward our mate, we will be beautiful in their sight and the marriage will be blessed.

Although intellectually we know what it takes to live for God, many are still vacillating between remaining in carnality and making a quantum leap into God's hands where their paths might seem less certain, all of which is uncomfortable to the flesh. The examples of individual choices that have been given in this chapter remind us of the pain that accompanies life outside of God's plan for our lives. Many Christians have made decisions without consulting God, and unfortunately are suffering from the consequences of doing so.

God wants to prevent women from making wrong decisions by using times of singleness to teach them how to be led by the Holy Spirit in every area of their lives. If you ask Him, God will heal the wounds you carry from old relationships and painful decisions made in the past to help you break the cycle of entering unlawful relationships when you become vulnerable to loneliness, despondency and heartache. Our walk with God is bitter and sweet, but He always rewards those who diligently seek Him and obey his commandments.

Lord, your word says that you will show me the path of life; in your presence there is fullness of joy and at your right hand are pleasures
for evermore (Psalm 16:11).
Strengthen my heart that I may weather the disappointments in life without sinning against you God. Send your sweet Holy Spirit to comfort me, to dry my tears when loneliness and distress creep upon me.

I know that you are a faithful God and you always honor your word.

If I delight myself in you, then you will grant this desire of my heart for a mate.

In the meantime, give me the strength to remain faithful to you.

Thank you for creating an escape from temptation

whenever I falter and consider succumbing to sinful pleasures,

or make wrong decisions.

Thank you for your Love, Grace and Mercy!

Amen.

Chapter 8

❧

DON'T MAKE GOD SPANK YOU

For whom the Lord loves, He corrects. (Proverbs 3:12)

Some of us learn things quickly, but for many of us, learning and growing can be a long, redundant process in which we keep making the same mistakes over and over again, until finally the proverbial little light in our heads makes us aware that we must desist old behaviors in order to experience the new changes we desire. The Holy Spirit serves as that 'little light' for those of us who truly seek to know truth. It was the Holy Spirit who finally caused me to shift my previous ideas on love and relationships in preparation for the marriage relationship I had prayed for. Thankfully, I was not allowed to enter into relationships that could have progressed into detrimental emotional situations; however, some of you might still be in unlawful relationships that you need to be released from before you can grow in your walk with God.

Many women hang on, and pray fervently that God will miraculously cause the man in their lives to love them so that the relationship will prosper, but something interesting happens when the Holy Spirit taps you on the shoulder to inform you that it is time for you to make a decision. It becomes clear that you can either choose to stew in the mess and sin you created in your life, and suffer at the hands of the devil, or decide to release all that is comfortable, all that is sinful, and experience complete freedom by following God on a path to eternal glory. Who wouldn't want God to make them free, you might ask? Who would not choose God over satan?

However, through our behaviors and thoughts, there are many times that we have chosen satan over God. There are some who continue to live together and fornicate, but attend church as a couple, somehow thinking that this act alone will compensate for their daily sinful lifestyles. Some have slept in on Sundays after a long Saturday night of carousing. Cursing at someone when angry, eating that fourth Krispy Kreme doughnut when you know it will make you sick, flipping off the driver that just cut you off on the freeway; there are a plethora of seemingly small choices we make on a daily basis that cater to the flesh that all qualify as sin, whether we want to admit it or not. Everything that is not of the spirit of God is a sin, and it is impossible to please God and live victoriously while living according to fleshly desires.

Romans 8:8 states, "So then those who are in the flesh cannot please God." There is no neutral ground between the world and God that can be tread upon. Worldly Christians suffer in their lives when they try to live in this gray area when God's word is written in unadulterated black and white. The Bible says, "For if you live according to the flesh you will die; but if by the Spirit you put to death the deeds of the body, you will live" (Romans 8:13). According to this verse, it can be surmised that there are indeed some good people, some water baptized Christians who will die, and not live in heaven because they still live after the flesh, but in John 8:51, Jesus says, "Most assuredly, I say to you, if anyone keeps My word he shall never see death." Before you can become God's girlfriend, or experience a deeper relationship with Jesus Christ, you must first make a decision to keep His commandments. Those who keep to the word of God cannot help but be blessed and live eternally, because those are the promises that are contained in the Bible.

With all that said, is the decision to live completely for God still a hard one for you to make? What or whom in this world could you desire to possess over the promises of God? When you hang on to the mess that hinders your spiritual growth, in essence you have chosen the trappings of the world over the promises of God.

It is also interesting to note that God will make provisions for those of us who are too weak or frightened to let go. Sometimes He will cause the people or circumstances around you to shift so as to force you to let go and run into His arms. For me, as I said, my phone stopped ringing. I could not get a date; then I experienced disappointment in my career plans and began to have financial problems. Why would all of these unpleasant circumstances befall me if God truly loved me, you might ask, if you have also experienced similar situations.

These things happened and might also happen to you <u>because</u> He loves you. I had gotten a little hard headed. I had found ways to meet new friends and to live with watching *Nick at Nite* on Saturday nights, so being single did not bother me as much. However, when other areas of my life seemed to crumble, and none of my creative solutions worked, I was forced to once again fall to my knees, fall out on the floor and fuss at God for not allowing me to prosper. As the psalmist cried out to God, "Before I was afflicted I went astray, but now I obey your word. You are good and what you do is good; teach me your decrees" (Psalm 119:67-68 NIV). God's discipline is not always about punishment, but is a tool He uses to bring us back within the hedges of His divine will.

God got my attention, but this time He kept it, and kept me talking to Him, because I finally realized that I could do nothing without Him. God has a way of making sinners run to Him, but He especially loves His children and will bring them back into the fold, like any good shepherd would, by any means necessary. If you have to lose a limb, a loved one, get laid off, or get swallowed by a big old fish before you submit to God, rest assured that even with all your infirmities, you will have to return to the fold, because He loves you that much. God will do whatever it takes to get your attention, but why make Him use drastic measures against you? Why not just come to God the first time He calls you?

I remember playing outside until the streetlights came on as a child. It was usually dark then, and all the kids in the neighborhood knew that it was time to go inside, but sometimes we were having so much fun that we pretended not to hear our mothers calling us. We continued like this until we saw our respective mothers physically come out of the house, walk to the end of the driveway, and yell, but by then we knew we were in trouble. We also knew we would have to answer the imminent question, "Didn't you hear me calling you?" With lowered heads and heaving chests from the run up the street, we would mumble something in response while trying to avoid a light smack.

As adults behaving as children, we play in the streets of the world, until a tragedy befalls us, then we see God. It is funny how some of us live day to day, mesmerized by sin, missing God in the pleasant simplicities of life, but see Him clearly during hard times. When these taxing circumstances occur, it is as if God has walked to the end of the driveway and asked, "Didn't you hear me calling you?"

As maturing Christians, we must stop blaming the devil for every bad thing that happens to us and accept the fact that we might have caused God to initiate some corrective measures against us. "For whom the Lord loves He corrects" (Proverbs 3:12). Likewise Adam and Eve tried to hide from God after they had committed sin. When God asked Adam, "Where art thou?" They knew they were in trouble and did not want to answer God, but when they did, like children, Adam blamed Eve and Eve blamed the serpent (Genesis 3:8-9; 12-13). Neither of them wanted to accept responsibility for their actions. Although God still loved them, he kicked them out of Eden, which equated to a spanking.

Just as we expect children to grow into adulthood and begin to accept responsibility for the decisions they make in their lives, likewise God expects us to develop into mature followers, who obey His word without having to be negatively motivated to do so.

God does not delight in the illnesses that many Christians suffer, but sometimes that is the only way some will heed his call. Lung cancer will motivate a smoker to quit. A wayward, or incarcerated child will make some parents seek God's direction for their lives, but how many of us praise God when a child smiles, or seek to know more of Him even after we have been promoted? God can and will get the glory out of situations that the devil might use to entrap us, and the messes we get ourselves into, due to our own human spirit and desires, but why should suffering be the inspiration for obeying God's commands? God speaks to us through his Word, and if we do not study the Bible and make ourselves aware of what He tells us about Himself and daily living, how will we ever be able to distinguish His voice from all the others trying to get our attention so that we can genuinely follow Him?

Basically much of what has been said in this chapter boils down to this simple plea: "Don't make God spank you." Answer Him the first time He calls you. Sometimes this is easier said than done, because heeding God's call might mean rejecting a proposal from an unGodly man, when you truly desire to be married. Heeding the call to life in the spirit is hard on the flesh, and it seems the fatter you are in sin, the longer it takes for the flesh to die.

When I finally got tired of trying to create my own success to no avail, exasperated, I finally said, "Well you do it then." God soon began to clear the obstructions from my life that had been choking the spiritual fruit He had sown. Paul expressed God's wishes toward the Ephesians, and all believers, when he prayed that the spirit of wisdom and revelation be upon them, so that the eyes of their understanding might be enlightened (Ephesians 1:17-18). God wants to build a relationship with those who love Him in order to impart spiritual knowledge and understanding of the inheritance they have in Him as His children. We understand that this symbiosis between us and God can only occur when we build a relationship with Jesus

Christ. Romans 5:1 reminds us that we have peace with God through Jesus Christ.

The children of Israel forced an eleven-day trip to the promised land of Canaan to become a forty-year ordeal. Unfortunately, not everyone who began the journey lived long enough to reap the rewards God had promised long before. Their lack of faith and immaturity made them grumble, moan, whine and complain about every little obstacle they encountered, even after God had spoken through Moses and produced sign after supernatural sign to prove His faithfulness to them. God exasperatedly asked Moses in Numbers 14:11 (KJV), "How long will this people provoke me? And how long will it be ere they believe me, for all the signs which I have shown among them?"

The Israelites rebelled against God so much that He literally ran out of patience with them and wanted to destroy the majority of them. Study for yourself the ungrateful attitudes and numerous accounts of disobedience that are attributed to them. God is not one that He should lie, so why is it difficult for us to walk in faith, and believe that God has a good plan for our lives that includes abundance and exceeding joy? If you truly desire to marry, why do you fear that God will somehow prohibit it?

In His word, God has promised us a life of victory and joy while on earth, our own promised lands, yet we, like the Israelites, distrust God when circumstances look grim. As a result, we attempt to create our own success, because it is easier to have faith in our own natural abilities, than the supernatural and all-powerful abilities of God.

Every time we decide not to pay tithes, because we cannot see how our bills can be paid without using 100% of our checks, (after taxes of course), or join a dating service for fear that God will not present us with a mate, we are telling God that we cannot trust Him enough to take control of our lives, despite the numerous times He has blessed us, and shown us how good and willing He is to provide us with the very best this earthly existence has to offer.

Maybe while still a babe in Christ, God seemed to act like your personal genie, where your every wish was His command. Every prayer was expediently answered. Like a spoiled child, you became accustomed to this egocentric relationship of ask and take, until God began to wean you and force you to become a mature Christian who is convinced of His faithfulness without Him having to prove it all the time. By weaning you, God is shaping you into the type of mature servant who will bless Him, in the midst of adversity, and who possesses a bulldog type faith that looks beyond circumstances to God who makes all things possible.

Be glad that our relationship with Jesus Christ gives us access to the love of God. "And not only that, but we also rejoice in God through our Lord Jesus Christ, through whom we have now received the reconciliation" (Romans 5:11). Jesus Christ shed His blood for our sins so that we could be free to receive and give the love of God to others. Because Jesus is our loving intercessor, we do not have to fear God's judgment. Having a relationship with Jesus means peace, love and liberty, but only if you keep His commandments. When the Holy Spirit begins to transform your mind into a more spiritual one, you will find that living God's way is not as hard as satan told you it would be.

However, before you can possess the land and inherit the kingdom, as the Israelites finally did, you must become a productive member of the body of Christ. God needs an army of overcoming Christians who trust Him and act like inheritors of His kingdom, not spoiled brats. This requires that your current carnal body and mental state be prepared to house the Holy Spirit of God. This preparation leads to the development of spiritual fruit, or the Christ-like character we need in order to have an abiding relationship with Jesus Christ. Before God can truly prepare our spirits to bear His fruit, however, he must perform an overhaul on our attitudes about hurtful past relationships, love and spirituality.

> *Dear God,*
> *Search my heart and reveal to me any hidden sins that I need to confess.*
> *I am ready to submit my life and thoughts to your will and word.*
>
> *Holy Spirit, bring to my attention any behaviors that do not please God,*

so that I can openly and honestly petition for your help to change.

There are areas of disobedience in my life that I want to faithfully surrender to
You, Heavenly Father.

Thank you for providing me with this opportunity to turn from my carnal ways and commit my life wholly to the Lord.

In the name of Jesus I thank you that it is done.
Amen.

Chapter 9

⊷

ATTITUDE ADJUSTMENT

By this My father is glorified, that you bear much fruit;
so you will be My disciples. (John 15:8)

I was trying to have a conversation with a friend of mine just after Serena Williams won the U. S. Tennis open in 1999. He had been screaming about her poor performance toward the end of the game, and I had begun to scrutinize her pronunciation while she gave post game interviews. He yelled at me, "She's just nervous. Have you ever been in that situation before?" "No," I shouted back. "But when I do get famous, I will always be able to speak well!" He said, "See that's why you won't be famous. You have the wrong attitude!" I did not appreciate that last comment, but it is true that your attitude will determine your success in the natural, as well as victory in your walk with God.

137

Likewise, before many singles can be married, the Holy Spirit must come in and clear out wrong thoughts, attitudes and behaviors concerning relationships. Actually this cleansing is God's way of building Christ-like character within you by removing that old emotional debris that accumulated in your heart over the years, and replacing it with the fruit of the Holy Spirit. The nine fruit of the spirit are listed in Galatians 5:22-23 (KJV), which reads, "But the fruit of the Spirit is love, joy, peace, longsuffering, gentleness, goodness, faith, Meekness, temperance: against such there is no law."

Before you can truly have a relationship with Jesus Christ, you must be stripped of unproductive thoughts or beliefs that hinder true fellowship with God. I mentioned before that I did not realize I had very much wrong with me, until the Holy Spirit lovingly revealed to me the strongholds that satan had built within my mind. Before the issues of my heart were revealed to me, I wanted so much for God to send me someone to love and marry, but since this prayer was not answered during the time this petition was heaviest on my heart, I began to doubt that God loved me enough to grant my prayer, which caused me to become bitter with God.

I could not fully fellowship with God while harboring these feelings. Because I could not hide my true feelings, I had to admit how I felt to God and ask for forgiveness. Just as in everyday relationships, God and I had to have some long talks and falling outs before our relationship could get back on track. Many of us do not realize how much God wants us to bring our broken selves to Him, with all of our baggage, so that He can lovingly heal us, and make us whole.

You can never "get right," or fix yourself before approaching God. Jude verse 24 (KJV), "Now unto him that is able to keep you from falling, and to present you faultless before the presence of his glory with exceeding joy," tells us that God is able to overlook our faults while we commune with Him. In fact, God is more than happy to do this for all who submit to Him. When I realized that God really enjoyed talking with little old me and would not condemn me for my sinful actions or thoughts, I began to talk to Him more often. Many of you need to reestablish your personal relationship with God, before

He can begin to reshape your character.

Now, remember, I am not writing as a new convert, but as an

experienced Christian. I officially accepted Christ by walking down

the aisle during Sunday School in my early teens, although I had

been heavily involved in church activities as a youth. I had an

appreciation for God and a holy fear, or reverence for Him, but the

personal relationship had begun to dwindle in my college years. All

that I had experienced up until this point in my life, had been

designed to bring me into intimate, loving relationship with Christ—

not one based upon material blessings, fear or signs and wonders,

but a relationship firmly entrenched in divine love.

THE PURGING

It is funny for me to recall when I became aware that I was

indeed developing spiritual fruit. It seems that my old junky

behaviors had to hit an all time peak before I realized I needed to

sincerely make a change. My cousin and uncle had come to visit another cousin of mine who practically lived down the street from me. My mother had given a care package to my uncle for me, so I went over to pick it up. I should add that I hardly ever saw this cousin and on three prior occasions before this visit, I had been mildly offended by her actions. On those three occasions, I saw her in public places and assumed she intentionally ignored me when she did not acknowledge me. So why didn't I just speak to her first, or call to let her know I had seen her out, but did not have the opportunity to speak to her? This would have been too logical of a resolution, and I was completely irrational during this pre-fruit period.

When I went over to pick up the package, I was mentally predisposed to become upset at anything she did that I did not like. Sure enough, when I walked through her door with my uncle to briefly say hello, she would not turn to acknowledge me, but this time, my uncle had witnessed her behavior, which made me feel justified in my anger. I was completely outdone and steamed, needless to say. I said nothing then; instead, I rushed home to call my mother and angrily recounted to her what had just happened. She tried to calm me down, but I told her that I was either going back over there, or call my cousin to have it out.

While in the throes of this vengeful spirit, I noticed that there was a book in the package by Joyce Meyer called *Managing Your Emotions*. That word came a little too late, because I was hot and wanted everyone to know it. I called my cousin and left what amounted to an invitation to a showdown on her recorder. Of course she accepted hours later when she finally returned home and got the message, but I refused to answer the phone. In fact, I blocked her number. She called from a different phone, but I still refused to answer, because my anger had subsided by this time.

Because my propensities to be quick tempered and to assume the worst about people and situations had to surface before they could be properly purged, it seemed that for two weeks after this episode with my cousin, I was engulfed in an emotional rampage like none I had experienced before. When I awoke in the mornings, I felt bad for no particular reason. During the day, I was short with people and even said some down right rude things to some, which was out of character for me. My flesh felt so uncomfortable that I would literally shift in my seat, or stand and shake around, as if doing these things would realign my skin with my spirit. My outside was out of balance with my inside. I could literally feel the resulting clash tingling along my flesh.

Some might have blamed this discomfort on oppression from the devil, but God's pruning process, or the ripping away of unGodly behaviors, thoughts and actions, is indeed a highly uncomfortable process to the flesh. Our natural selves cannot understand spiritual law, which dictates that everything in our lives must go haywire, in order to gain and understand peace. God was preparing me for the further enlightenment the Holy Spirit was going to give me concerning my life and relationship with Jesus Christ, but before I could receive this spiritual information, my natural self had to become absolutely uncomfortable and displeased with the fleshly state I was in.

Maybe many of you need to also realize that God cannot pour his Holy Spirit out upon the junk of the flesh. No good thing dwells within any of our flesh, as Paul attested to in Romans 7:18; therefore, because God is holy, He cannot truly use us through his Holy Spirit, until we begin to live spiritually. If you have not received the gifts of the Holy Spirit that we have been promised, such as speaking in tongues, or operating in the word of knowledge, it might just be that you still have sinful areas in your life that God has to excavate before you can move forward in His power.

The natural man cannot receive spiritual understanding; therefore your flesh has to be cleansed and purged before you can mature further in your relationship with Jesus Christ. In John 15:2 Jesus states, "Every branch in Me that does not bear fruit He takes away, and every branch that bears fruit, He prunes that it may bear more fruit." Just as in the natural when farmers or gardeners burn the land, strip trees, or pull weeds to ensure that new growth will occur, Jesus is purged and purges us, not to anger or destroy us, but to make sure that our fruit reproduces.

A tree cannot allow the fruit that grows from it to remain on the branches, because the health and nurturing capabilities of the branch will be compromised. The fruit must fall or be gathered by those who can benefit from it, so that the next round of fruit can also be nurtured. So it is with our spiritual fruit. We must continually give to others the peace, love, joy, temperance, etc. that has grown within us to ensure that the cycle of fruit bearing will remain strong and healthy within our lives. "By this is My Father glorified, that you bear much fruit; so will you be My disciples" (John 15:8). God gets the glory when others see the evidence of spiritual fruit within us, which makes it that much more important for us to always exhibit the fruit of the spirit.

I finally realized I had to gain control of my emotions when I behaved in such a way toward my former soulmate that made him not want to deal with my sporadic moods anymore. Although PMS is a very real, behavior-altering period in women's lives, this phenomenon does not give them license to be emotionally erratic and mean, especially to loved ones. Not everyone who has felt your wrath will be so quick to forgive you, once you have decided to apologize, hoping to continue as normal, until the next PMS period comes along. I had to personally understand that sometimes I acted this way toward people even when it was not that time of the month. These reactionary moments began in my life as a young adult, which is why I frequently blamed it on PMS.

My proclivity to become emotionally unstable was in direct conflict with the fruit of peace, longsuffering, gentleness and temperance. I often justified those occasional outbursts by telling myself that I was simply confronting the problem and releasing the negative emotions it wrought before I imploded or became otherwise stressed out. For years, pop psychologists have admonished Americans, especially women, to get in touch with their feelings, which is not a bad thing to do, if done under divine guidance. However, God wants us to always be governed by the Holy Spirit and to abide in the fruit of peace.

THE PURPOSE

In order to walk in the spirit, we must abide in Christ, the true vine, His Word (John 15:5-7), and be filled with the Holy Ghost. If we cultivate our relationship with Christ according to these three principles, we will be less likely to act and react in a fleshly manner. Because the flesh and the spirit are opponents, if we walk in the spirit we will not fulfill the lust of the flesh (Galatians 5:16). Since we can only do one or the other at any given moment, we must consciously choose to walk in the spirit every moment of the day.

When we mature in Christ and our fruit produces on a regular basis, we are in prime position to receive all the blessings and petitions we have asked of God. Notice that almost every scripture that promises us we can have anything we want is conditional, meaning that we have to perform an action or meet certain criteria before the promises can be released to us. For example, I John 5:14-15 tells us that we can be confident that God will grant our petitions if we ask according to His will, which nullifies our own fleshly desires. Can you really expect God to give you a new Lexus if your latent desire is to upstage your neighbor? God's will is not selfish and neither should be our requests.

To abide in Christ and allow His word to abide in you are the two conditions to receiving the blessings of God that appear in John 15:7. Malachi 3:10 tells believers to pay tithes so that God can open the windows of heaven unto them. There are many such conditional promises in the Bible that we should diligently seek through increased study so that we can understand exactly how to be blessed and live victoriously. The more we grow up in God, the less He will spoon feed us, because we have to learn how to walk and live according to his will, just as infants progress from milk to solid food.

The fruit that God develops within us is not only essential to our relationship with Jesus, but to our daily, personal relationships as well. Therefore, as singles who desire to be married, we must practice living according to the spirit before we enter the marriage relationship we desire. Who would want to live with someone who seemed upset all the time, or became irritated at the least little thing?

How can we even think of bringing children into the relationship if we do not first practice the patience that is critical to child rearing?

I truly believe that marriages can last forever if both people are mature Christians who love God and are filled with His spirit. Therefore, relationships, whether they are with potential mates, parents, or friends, do not have to be hard work if you bring God into those relationships. Some of us, however, have not gotten that far in our journeys with Christ and are still pursuing and leaving relationships according to the worldly thoughts, attitudes and behaviors that we have accumulated over the years, even when we thought we were serving God.

The spirit revealed to me that I had developed a wrong attitude about relationships with men due to the disappointment and frustration I had encountered on the dating scene. I thought I was all right, but I had not been honest with myself about the way I really felt about men and marriage track relationships. I still liked men and still wanted one, but I had gotten a bit jaded about finding the right one. Like Ally McBeal, I had begun to seriously doubt that there was a Mr. Right for me. Obviously there was for some, since women marry almost every day, but not for me. In fact, a male colleague of mine told me that it seemed I had adopted a defeatist attitude, which embarrassed me into wanting to change, because I did not want to be perceived as a beaten woman in the game of love and marriage.

The next chapter outlines some of the old attitudes and behaviors many women adopt while playing the dating game. Realize that you will need to undergo God's pruning process before you receive the relationship you desire. It might take longer than you would like, and it might seem that you are the only one of your friends who is still not married and having children, but be blessed in knowing that your family relationship will prosper because of the spiritual renewal God has favored you with.

> *O Lord, you have searched me and you know me.*
> *You know when I sit and when I rise; you perceive my*
> *thoughts from afar.*
> *You discern my going out and my lying down; you are*
> *familiar with all my ways.*

Before a word is on my tongue you know it completely, O Lord.

You hem me in - behind and before; you have laid your hand upon me.

Such knowledge is too wonderful for me, too lofty for me to attain.

(Psalm 139:1-6 NIV)

Thank you for searching me Lord and finding me good!

Amen.

Chapter 10

❧

LET IT ALL BLOW

Therefore, if anyone is in Christ, he is a new creation; old things have passed away; behold, all things have become new. (II Corinthians 5:17)

DISAPPOINTMENT IN PROMISING RELATIONSHIPS

While I was actively dating, I met some guys I had much in common with and assumed that a relationship with them was inevitable. We had good conversations. In fact, most of them had given me work, home, cellular, pager, every number they could be reached by, which demonstrated how interested in me they were, so I thought. Since they were so eager to be contacted by me, I assumed that they had no girlfriend or wife and were pursuing me for that purpose. They were all attractive and fun guys. Most of them had invited me to their homes. In some cases, I was even introduced to family members. I had every reason to expect to have a relationship with these guys, but after about two weeks, they would stop calling me.

I refused to call them to ask why, but in one case I did. That guy told me that he really did like me, but was not ready for the committed relationship he perceived I wanted. I thanked him for being honest and open with me, because I was then able to stop questioning whether or not I was good relationship material. However, because a few others after him had also disappeared in similar fashion, I began to think that I had about a two-week shelf life with the guys I went out with.

As a result, when I did meet someone I liked, I remained distant, because I assumed that they would be gone in about two weeks. After having had my fill of this type disappointment, I decided to stop putting myself in a position to be met for a while. As long as I entertained the thought that a potential prospect would leave in two weeks, I would continue to behave in ways that would in fact make him leave, even if he had no intentions to do so.

Everyone expresses disappointment in different ways, especially when it comes to relationships. Some get angry, violent, depressed, or passive about the situation. Many women compromise their emotions, bodies, finances, and spiritualities in efforts to avoid dealing with rejection or loneliness. God showed me that if I delighted myself in Him that I would never have to be brokenhearted. In Luke 4:18, Jesus says that He came to heal the brokenhearted and give freedom to the oppressed. Meditating on this scripture brought peace and healing to my battered emotions.

However, before I received this healing, I had to deal directly with some emotional strongholds about men and relationships that had affected my attitude and dealings with everyone in my life, not just men, but especially men that I encountered in a variety of social and professional situations. Remember that emotional wounds in one area of your life, regardless of what they are, will affect your entire life, just as a cold is not simply an isolated illness, but a virus that invades the whole body. Likewise, spiritually unhealthy thoughts about relationships must be uprooted and healed, because they will affect your relationship with Jesus Christ and everyone else in your life.

ANGER OR FEAR OF REJECTION

Like many other women, whenever a guy chose not to communicate with me anymore, I felt inferior in some way and assumed that he left me for another woman. I stopped talking to guys for a while because I was afraid that they would find fault in me and leave. Fear is the root for many of our erratic behaviors. We become extremely accommodating to some who do not deserve our efforts for fear of being rejected if we do not make them like us.

As is more common with women who feel scorned by men, I too became angry sometimes and thought of becoming a fatal attraction to prove to them that I could not simply be dismissed from their lives. In the end, I had too much pride to stoop so low, although many women have. I do recall bugging a guy to death until he got his phone number changed, because I assumed he had chosen another female over me. When Jesus became my boyfriend, however, it became crystal clear to me that he would never leave me nor forsake me and had chosen me before the foundations of the world to be with Him (Ephesians 1:4). With this kind of love and acceptance from the head of all principality and power (Colossians 2:10), I realized that I never had to fear or become angry at perceived rejection from others, especially men.

FEELINGS OF INADEQUACY

Because I had been disappointed and felt rejected at times by men, I consequently began to feel as if I was an inadequate potential marriage partner, based upon my past dating track record. I began to look more closely at the appearances of other women, and to question whether or not I was pretty enough. I scrutinized my face in the mirror every morning and decided that if my nose was slimmer, I could have any man I wanted. I then decided that I needed to wear the type of sophisticated clothes I could not afford, because men responded better to designer women.

Maybe my makeup was not heavy enough? Men seemed to prefer more animated looking women as opposed to the wash and go natural looking woman. I had already lost as much weight as I desired to, but maybe I was not toned enough, like all those bouncy women on television fitness programs. Basically, I began to look for reasons for not being good enough for men to settle down with. My attitude? I knew I needed more work on that, but for the most part, men told me they liked my personality and sense of humor.

Unfortunately, many women also buy into satan's lies and even go so far as to attempt suicide, plagued by thoughts of not measuring up to society's standards of success and attractiveness. There is a long list of entertainers, authors, mothers and fathers who destroyed themselves, because they failed to realize that even with all their frailties and shortcomings, they were beloved children of God. Unfortunately, man has created an image of God as a judgment-wielding martinet, instead of the unconditional, loving spirit that He is, and satan has craftily learned how to capitalize on our misconceptions of love and forgiveness.

Those feelings of inadequacy I experienced did not last long, however. Every time a guy winked at me, or whispered a passing compliment, I felt more convinced that I was still cute! More importantly, I digested Psalm 139, which reminds us that we have been marvelously and beautifully created in God's image.

THERE ARE NO AVAILABLE GOOD MEN

This seems to be the battle cry of many women who are entering the 21st century unmarried and without families of their own. There is an element of comfort in projecting your single status on the fact that all the good men are already married, incarcerated, or just not interested in women. As I got more involved in local activities, it seemed I began to meet more men who belonged to other women, either formally by marriage, or informally as live-ins.

As a result, I did think that less deserving women had already taken all the men who were good for me. Oh, yes, I became critical of women who seemed to have decent-looking, caring men to go home to. Sometimes I gauged their attractiveness against mine and determined that I was better looking and better educated. I sighed

over how unfortunate it was that I was not around when their men

were seeking women to marry. Oh yes. In the dog eat dog world of

dating and mating, women begin to viciously compare themselves

with the competition to either affirm or enhance what they have to

offer. However, the more I began to have faith in God, as Mark 11:22

admonishes, I became convinced that He would bring the right man

to me, even if He had to create another Adam to keep His covenant

with me!

FEAR OF BEING ALONE

After reading Genesis 2:18, "And the Lord God said, it is not

good that the man should be alone; I will make him an help meet for

him," I remember asking God if he had forgotten that I, a *wo*-man,

still did not have a partner. In fact, I inserted my name in place of

"the man" to reiterate to God the fact that it was not good for me to

still be alone either. Satan tried to convince me that I would be single

forever, because God just did not want me to have a husband. I eventually was able to combat this lie with the knowledge that God advocates and sanctifies marriage. Although everyone will not choose to be married, marriage, as an institution of God, lies within the will He has for those who follow Him, as verified in Hebrews 13:4, "Marriage is honorable among all, and the bed undefiled; but fornicators and adulterers God will judge."

If God has promised us in Matthew 28:20 that He will be with us, even unto the end of the world, why then do many of us allow the root fear of being alone to govern our actions? We are often afraid to make radical changes in our lives, because we are afraid of failure. Both males and females have remained in unGodly relationships for fear of having to start all over again with a new person. In fact, many of us are afraid to let the Holy Spirit have His way in our lives, because we are afraid to make a quantum leap from the world into the hands of God who loves us. There are many Christian single parents out there who run from relationship to relationship, trying to find someone to fill a parental void for fear of raising children alone, despite the fact that God has told them that their sins are forgiven and He will never forsake them. Many of us need to understand that when we act out of fear, we cannot walk in faith, without which, it is impossible to please God.

GOD WANTS ME SINGLE

Since it is apparent that God's will includes marriage for those willing to accept this ministry, there should be no question as to whether God desires for you to marry. The choice to marry is an individual one. Since marriage is honorable, and God does not withhold good gifts from his children, then He is not the one keeping you single—you are! If you truly had the Pauline gifts of celibacy and singleness, you would not be reading this book. In fact, you would not even have the slightest desire to marry or to have a family. Now that you understand your responsibility for your single state, you are now open to learning the exact reasons why from the Holy Spirit. It is my belief that everyone is single for a reason, especially those who are over forty and are still waiting for God to send a mate their way. The Holy Spirit will let you know if you are unmarried due to a personal fault, or issue that needs to be dealt with, or if it is simply a matter of God's timing.

It is important to understand that God uses periods of singleness to teach us about our true spiritual selves, to purge and deliver us from the satanic influence of our worldly lifestyles, to settle our hearts and minds, and to draw us into deeper relationship with Him, so that we can experience true, divine love and learn to extend that to others. God does not punish us with singleness. The closer we draw nearer to God, the more we realize how our own words will bring life or death to different areas of our lives. For example, if a person declares that he will always be broke and never make enough money, he will remain poor. Likewise, if a woman declares she does not need a man—even in jest—then she will not have one. These are more than self-fulfilling prophecies, because there are numerous scriptures that inform us of the power God has embedded into the words of believers, so that we either have what we say, or choke what we desire to have with vain, negative words.

Needless to say, I had to be purged of all the ideas that produced wrong thinking and attitudes about relationships, because such thoughts precluded me from fully trusting and opening up to God. I wanted to change and I wanted to have a heart to worship God, but because these strongholds had developed in my mind, I could not love or trust in the Lord with all my heart.

This hardness and isolation from God can throw you into a valley of depression, and make you feel that life is drudgery, but when God touches you in that valley, an inexplicable sweetness will fall upon every area of your life. You will run and not become weary, walk and not faint, even when it looks like you have every reason to just lie down and call it quits. God loves us enough to renew us, not just to make us feel better, but to enable us to maintain victory in our lives.

So when you pray and whine for a husband, do not expect for a man to fall from the sky with a big red bow and a tag that reads, "From God With Love." Instead, expect to become a better, more enlightened person than you have ever been. When it finally dawned on me about a year later that God heard me and was indeed making me husband ready, I knew that the next relationship I entered would be a more spiritual one. I had become a more spiritual minded person, which meant that I would also leave all the little silly man-woman relationship games behind.

OLD DATING GAMES

Everyone has done something to either create of deflect interest in a potential mate. Some of us have left little cutesy, "just calling to say hello" messages on someone's recorder. One guy used to sing Al Green songs on my recorder, which I thoroughly enjoyed, but when we do these things to compete with another prospect, then it becomes a silly little game that we should not be forced to play in the kingdom of God.

How about the old pretending not to show someone you like them for fear that they will perceive this as an opportunity to take advantage of you game? Or the granddaddy of them all, especially for young women - the old, sleep with him to get a relationship started, retarded, pathetic game? I personally engaged in the "make his life miserable" game when a guy stopped seeing me, by leaving excessive messages, or saying rude things to him before he took off for good. Lastly, many have either swiped or otherwise kept a personal item from a former boyfriend or girlfriend, and used that as an excuse to see him or her again. The old, "You left your CD over here, do you still want it?" game.

These games that we have played at one time or the other establishes the fact that we need to be purged of worldly behaviors, as well as attitudes. When the Holy Spirit becomes your best friend, and you talk with Him on a regular basis, you cannot help but to think and act according to the loving truth he replaces that old junky stuff with. Although I still did not have a boyfriend, and still pretty much watched *I Love Lucy* reruns every Saturday night, I felt all right with just having the Holy Spirit accompany me wherever I went. I realized that I still had friends that I could talk with, but I often chose to read the Bible, or to have an all out conversation with the Holy Spirit. Sometimes I would not talk about the single life, because I had moved on to other areas of my life that I needed guidance on. I began to feel that I had spent too much time whining about being without a mate, so I decided to exert some of that energy onto other projects.

Oh yes, I still felt pangs of yearning when I saw couples holding hands, or sharing a laugh, especially when I saw homeless couples traversing here and there with one another, but I felt more ready and confident about relationships than I had ever felt. At last, my relationship with Christ had been restored to the point where I could hear the Holy Spirit talking to me, which reassured me that I was becoming the type of victorious Christian He wanted me to be.

I still had to fight bouts of faithlessness and melancholy with satan, but I now had the power to resist the temptation to once again feel defeated. As James 4:7 states, "Submit yourselves therefore to God. Resist the devil, and he will flee from you." When you begin to read and memorize scripture, you equip yourself with the ammunition necessary to quench the fiery darts of the enemy (Ephesians 6:16-17). The more I learned of the love and promises of God, the more my faith grew, even amidst unfavorable circumstances.

The mental tribulation I had endured, that fully began when I became dismayed about my single status, had actually wrought hope in God, versus despair. Hope can be defined as having confident expectations. Exercising faith and hope taught me that God would deliver on every petition I had set before Him. As a result, the love of God abounded in my heart, which led to an exhilarating experience in the spirit (Romans 5: 4-5).

Thank you Lord that your word is a balm to my soul;
a love letter engrafted upon my heart.

Surely in my sweet communion with you,
I hear these words dance lightly in my ear:
"How beautiful you are, my beloved, how beautiful!
Your eyes behind your veil are like doves.

You are so beautiful, my beloved, so perfect in every part.
You are like a private garden, my treasure, my bride!
You are like a spring that no one else can drink from, a fountain of my own.
You are like a lovely orchard bearing precious fruit, with the rarest of perfumes: nard and saffron, calamus and

cinnamon, myrrh and aloes, perfume from every incense tree, and every other lovely spice.

You are a garden fountain, a well of living water, as refreshing as the streams from the Lebanon mountains."

(Song of Solomon 4:1, 7, 12-15 NLT)

Amen.

Chapter 11

ক্ট

WHEN JESUS BECAME MY BOYFRIEND

*Jesus said to him, "You shall love the Lord God with
all your heart,
with all your soul, and with all your mind."
(Matthew 22:37)*

I cannot explain how it happened, or how it felt to be freed from issues that had plagued me as a single woman. The more I studied the Bible and had uninhibited conversations with the Holy Spirit, the more free I became. The Spirit became my best friend, because He was the only one I trusted enough to talk to about the concerns of my heart. As I have said many times already, my phone did not ring and I still stayed home every Friday and Saturday night crying about not having a satisfying social life. I prayed, read the word and had falling out, "I can't go on" fits for several months.

I finally realized that my solitude was not a punishment, but necessary to my spiritual development in a way that I did not quite understand at first. Then it dawned on me that I could not attribute the peace I felt to anyone but God. God wanted me to know without a doubt that it was He who was strengthening me and refashioning me. I could not take credit for this renewal in any way, because I had run out of my human ability to even get up in the morning. No earthly friend was there to encourage me and on the two occasions I did try to open up to two good friends, I realized that they could not understand the spiritual tug of war and stretching I had been enduring. I was totally dependent upon the Holy Spirit to teach me and empower me to live daily. I began to hear the Holy Spirit more when I finally reached this level of dependency, which is the type of close relationship He wants to have with us.

During this intense period of spiritual sequester, I found it difficult, but not impossible, to continue even a telephone friendship with male and female acquaintances I had known before my spiritual renovation. It seemed that everything and everyone that was not spiritual, or enlightened through the Holy Spirit, had to be taken from me for a while. I was encased in a spiritual cocoon God had spun especially for me, and a premature break from this secret place would have meant the demise of the spiritual strength I had gained to that point. Although I did not like what I perceived as extreme isolation, I thanked God for creating a new creature within me.

Some expect to become a new creature in Christ as soon as they are baptized, or sincerely confess a belief in Jesus Christ, but this metamorphosis did not occur for me until months before the new millennium. Still, others might think that it is necessary to be drugged out, or near death to have a life altering moment with God, but this is not true. It is quite true that those who have been delivered from much, love God that much more. However, if you have been mentally oppressed, and are now free, I guarantee you that you have just as, if not an even more powerful testimony than those Christians who have been delivered from other severe circumstances. In fact, the emotional baggage that many of us carry destroys our lives in more significant ways than any drug or illness can. Emotional distress can be as equally destructive, because it steals your joy and zeal for living, which can make you feel like the walking dead, until your fellowship with Jesus Christ is strengthened.

James 4:8 admonishes Christians to draw nigh to God so that He can draw nigh to them. The more I made an effort to know God, the more unburdened I felt. I took baby steps toward God, and he carried me, dragged me and pushed me along in my walk with Him. No matter how I stumbled, the point is that I kept moving forward in faith, with God's help.

When Jesus became my boyfriend, it was as if I had entered a realm of truth that allowed me to look at my old self, who was a good person, but powerless against the oppressions of the devil. Instead of fighting back, the old me laid helpless under the mental pummeling of satan's lies. The devil told me I would always be single and would probably die in the new millennium alone. Unfortunately, the old me listened to that negative talk long enough to be oppressed and depressed by it, until God said it was time for a new, more powerful me to come forth. I had been powerless because my relationship with Jesus was weak. Since I read the word inconsistently, I did not have the spiritual weapons needed to defend myself against the attacks of satan.

While in my cocoon, gaining strength, the Holy Spirit revealed to me how the devil had tried to use my own mind to destroy me. The saying "the battle is in the mind" is not a cliché, but a truth, especially for those who are involved in more cerebral occupations, like teaching. II Corinthians 10:5 tells us how to gain victory within our minds. We are to bring all thoughts into the captivity, or subjection of Jesus Christ by becoming obedient to His word.

A TOUCH FROM GOD

One Sunday, the Spirit touched me in a way I had not known before. Although I tend to be a rather conservative worshipper in public, on this day, I cried and praised God with all my heart. This was significant, because although I had routinely attended church, I had not felt His love abounding in my heart because of the strongholds that had previously prohibited me. Even in the car on the way home, I continued to cry, "Thank you Jesus!" When I entered my apartment, the Spirit directed me to get rid of some items I had not even used or thought about in a long while. I did not ask questions. I simply took those things to the dumpster and felt completely released. Shortly afterward, I heard some things in my spirit I almost giggled at in unbelief, but readily accepted. Inwardly I giggled, "Me? Ashan Hampton?" but the new me was prepared to receive whatever God told me.

I felt better about life, and although I still had my little moments, I had faith enough to believe that everything I had prayed for would come to pass. A friend I had not seen in some time told me I seemed more relaxed. I was tempted to ask how I was before, but I knew the answer, and was aware that a remarkable change had indeed come over me.

Although I still truly desired to be in a relationship, I did not set out to scout my congregation or otherwise meet potential prospects like I had before. I was also able to understand exactly why I could not have married any of the guys I had deemed future husbands.

Spending my 28th birthday practically alone, again, was hard, but I kept repeating all the scriptures I had memorized concerning faith. I put my marriage partner wish list away for a while and concentrated on fortifying my relationship with Jesus Christ through prayerful conversations and studying the word. I mean really studying, not simply reading. Many pages of my Bible are dog-eared, highlighted and have annotations written along the margins, because I had to aggressively know the word. During this time, I also continued to practice sexual abstinence.

A HIGH MAINTENANCE RELATIONSHIP

It was at this time that I superimposed my natural idea of a relationship upon the one that now existed between Jesus and me. If I could function consistently in a relationship with Jesus, then I knew I would be properly prepared for the man God would send my way. These are the questions I used to assess my relationship with Jesus Christ.

1. Have you told Him how much you love Him?

2. Have you taken care of your financial responsibilities by paying tithes?

3. Have you been faithful to God, cherishing Him above all else?

4. Have you remained sexually pure?

5. Have you been out on a date with God lately?

6. Have you told someone what your boyfriend Jesus did for you today?

7. Have you discussed daily life decisions with Him?

8. Are you listening to what God is saying to you?

If you look at this list, you can discern what secular relationship experts have deemed the cornerstones of effective communication that are necessary for maintaining a successful relationship. Questions one and six deal with showing appreciation for your spouse and voicing that to others. Being financially responsible and debt free often eliminates potential strain on a relationship in the natural, and the spiritual as well. How? Because your prayers will cease to become gripe sessions about money problems, and will hence become more pure and meaningful. Fidelity is the key to developing trust in natural relationships, which translates into sexual purity in our relationship with Jesus Christ. Our jobs, cars, children, pets, or whatever else we might hold dear in this life, cannot be placed above the affection we give to God. This list also includes fornication, or other means of sexual satisfaction.

The purpose of going out on dates with a potential partner is to get to know that person. Likewise, attending church conferences, tent revivals or any such activities provide a forum to spend time with God. Whenever I went to a movie, or any place alone, I would say, "Come on God we're going to a movie, or to get a Krispy Kreme doughnut." God wants to be involved in every aspect of your life. I almost thought I was getting a bit carried away when I asked God about every little thing, like, should I go to Publix or Cub Foods to buy *Ben & Jerry's* ice cream, but I would often find that ice cream on sale when I asked for God's direction! When it comes to God, I do not think we can go overboard in serving Him and involving Him in our lives. Lastly, the world has become such an aficionado of communication. Whenever someone speaks of interacting with other human beings, communication is esteemed as key to such successful interaction, just as prayer constitutes our communication with God.

Jesus was my boyfriend now. I had a better perception of myself as a child of God and probably looked better physically. They say a woman in love, or whom a man cares for has a certain glow about her, and so should a woman who is involved with God. With this rationale, I became more careful of my physical appearance. I made sure my hair looked cute and that the polish on my toenails matched my fingernails. I resumed an exercise regiment and used more herbal health products. I had undergone an extensive spiritual cleansing that I wanted to maintain from the inside out.

Did I miraculously adopt a saintly air, or a desire to join the Peace Corps? No, but the changes that had occurred in my thinking became noticeable in other areas of my life. Was my faith now so strong that I never doubted God? No. Remember that developing a relationship with Jesus Christ is a process, and the success of this relationship depends upon the decisions you make. God will not make you supernaturally perform for Him like a marionette. The Holy Spirit is a gentleman who will not force His way into your life. You have to sincerely ask and invite Him into your life as Jesus states in Revelation 3:20. "Behold, I stand at the door and knock. If anyone hears My voice and opens the door, I will come in to him and dine with him, and he with Me."

Matthew 7:7 applies not only to material items we want to receive, but to the Holy Spirit also. Ask and you will receive His presence; seek and He will reveal Himself to you; knock, and the door, which is Jesus Christ, will be opened unto you. In a nutshell, when you decide that you want to have a personal relationship with Jesus Christ, all you have to do is ask, seek and knock.

Although I had become stronger spiritually, I still had moments in the natural when being single, without a boyfriend, or even a date, bothered me. Through these moments, I read the Bible, and talked with other young women who also sought marriage relationships. They in turn inspired me to keep the faith, believing that God would keep covenant with me by granting this desire of my heart.

Heavenly Father,

Thank you for being everything to me, even the love of my life.

It is amazing how you reveal yourself to me differently in relation to the events of my life.

I have seen you act as a friend, a father, a counselor, and a gentle lover;

So many expressions of your personality I could name.

You have fulfilled so many needs in my life, yet remained the same.

What an amazing, glorious, living God I serve!

All praises be to God almighty!

Amen.

Chapter 12

❧

KEEPING THE FAITH

Now may the God of hope fill you with all joy and peace in believing, that you may abound in hope by the power of the Holy Spirit. (Romans 15:13)

Some women eat, some sulk, some are overtaken by fits of crying or insomnia, but when I am in a 'mood,' (experiencing mild bouts of depression), I sometimes buy unnecessary stuff and chocolate; miscellaneous items I never use on a consistent basis, but which at the moment of purchase, distracts me from thinking about my problems. A little while after my high experience in the spirit, I came back down to a valley and began to once again collect fitness videos. A few years ago, when I made a concerted effort to lose weight, I bought the complete Tamilee Webb *Buns of Steel* series: *Buns of Steel*

5, Thighs of Steel, Abs of Steel, Buns of Steel 7, Arms & Abs of Steel and

Buns of Steel 2000 featuring Donna Richards.

Then of course I needed more fitness equipment to vary the workouts so that I could overcome the weight loss plateau I was sure to hit. So, piece by piece I added a cute, grape-colored jump rope, a set of white five pound weights, a green set of ten pound weights, a gray set of twenty, a junior dumbbell set, the ever popular Brenda Dykgraaf grape-colored *Ab Roller*, a grape-colored Denise Austin aerobic step with adjustable heights, and Suzanne Sommers' infamous *Thigh Master Plus*, with three adjustable tension settings, and a blue set of ankle weights.

One day, as I schlepped through the *Target* superstore that had just opened near my house, I felt inspired to buy a bag of *Dove's Promises* milk chocolate with little affirmations printed inside the wrappers, and to buy the last video that completed my Denise Austin *Hit the Spot* series. Now my arms, bust, abs, thighs and buns could be as firm as Denise's still are well into her forties. At this point, I was feeling a little low, but had not quite hit rock bottom. For women, the consumption of chocolate is usually a big signal that a low moment is just around the corner. I felt myself slipping, but could not stop myself from slipping into the "Why don't I have a man yet?" valley that I thought I had conquered some time ago.

Although Jesus had become my boyfriend, and things were going well between us, I still longed to have a mortal man in my life who would call me on the telephone to ask me out for a date; we would shortly fall in love and praise God that we had found each other. I still hung on to this, what some would call a fantasy, but in my mind, it had become part of the vision I had for my life. Because I could see a marriage relationship in the plan for my life, I became more anxious about grasping it. I became upset when I realized that I could not impatiently catapult myself into that area of my life, but instead, I had to patiently allow God to prepare me to receive that blessing. The waiting got hard; so I bought chocolate, fitness videos and called a few single friends of mine to receive whatever encouragement from them I could.

I could not call the top two friends I normally would have during this funk I was experiencing, because they had become pregnant and were dealing with issues concerning being a single parent that I could not relate to. It was difficult for me to congratulate them, because I understood the psychology behind their circumstances. They had also grown tired of waiting for God to direct them toward their mate, so they settled for men who were in their immediate view.

Their pregnancies, whether they realized it or not, became a spiritual lesson for them that taught them the consequences of not seeking God during a time when they were the most vulnerable to loneliness and to their human spirits. Having children is a beautiful thing, but having them out of context to God's divine order of things is not honorable; however, because we have seen God grant second chances to single parents by providing them with a mate to help them establish a family unit, many young women have come to believe that there is nothing wrong with having children outside of marriage, or in some cases, without the involvement of a man in the procreation process.

Because God is a God of love and restoration, I have no doubt that my friends will prosper; however, witnessing single parents find loving relationships can become a bone of contention for us single women who are diligently seeking God's will for our lives prior to marriage. We get a little upset sometimes when a nice looking, eligible man has taken up with a woman with two or more children. During those moments, I began to question if God really was working in my life. If so, then how could He allow this woman to have exactly what I most desire when she has not undergone any spiritual work?

I got upset with God on more than one occasion because of what I perceived as the wicked collecting the blessings I was more prepared to receive. Those old doubts and pangs of loneliness crept upon me even after my big boyfriend experience with God. I wish I could tell you that all became rosy in my life and I was transformed into this perfect, faith filled child of God, but that is not what happened for me. Although I had become stronger in the spirit, I still had to deal with the impatience of my flesh.

Realize that satan wants to attack your faith and commitment to God through discouragement and depression. You literally must fight daily to maintain the spiritual progress you have made with God. I stopped condemning myself when I realized that my doubts were really not from my heart, but from the imps of hell that wanted to knock me off God's path, back into the oppressive hole satan once had me bound in.

I could not stop the thoughts from coming, but I could rebuke them with every scripture I could think of regarding God's faithfulness. The closer you get to receiving your blessings, the stronger the enemy's attacks will become, which means you must increase your spiritual arsenal. I could not afford to slack off on studying the word and submitting myself to God through prayer, but I had.

In order to keep the faith, you must stay vigilant against the enemy's attacks by consistently confessing scripture and talking to

God in prayer. Although I do get on my knees to pray formally, the majority of the time I have conversations with the Holy Spirit just as I would with a friend over the telephone. He speaks back to me, but particularly when I am studying the word. I receive the most enlightenment when I am actually reading the Bible. We cannot become so busy, or overwhelmed with our lives that we forget to read what God is saying to us. Remember that the word of God is the sword of the spirit and is our best weapon against satan's attempts to make us lose faith in God.

As I said before, I tried to receive comfort from some of my friends who were still single. I called a recently divorced friend of mine. We discussed our most recent male friends and I whined to her about how much I wanted to get married at least once. She believed that she would find the right one, and that I would too, but she still had someone to go out with and I did not. She had a male friend to call when she got a little lonely, and I, like a knucklehead, began to ask God why I did not have 'meantime boyfriends' like that. I had to remind myself that I had asked for a husband, not a temporary warm body. Needless to say, I did not become very encouraged by her.

I tried to call the friend girl I complained to about men in Atlanta, but she had also found a boyfriend. She was very involved with his parents, his children, his baggage, basically. It was a bit difficult to talk to her anyway, because she had not begun the process of committing herself to God as I had done.

When I could not find anyone adequate enough to relay my distress to, I once again fussed at God about how much I really wanted to live for Him, but that it was taking a little too long for Him to come through for me. I complained about not having any spiritually mature friends to confide in. I told Him everything I had on my heart to tell. I once again felt low, like I could not go on, but then an amazing thing happened. After all the crying and fussing, I jumped right back up, began to read an inspirational book and to clean my apartment. I continued on like I had never even fallen out on the floor. God's love is everlasting, and thankfully, once He has begun a work in you, He will see it through to the end, if you continue to cooperate.

God knew that when I fell out, it was due to frustration in not being able to think His thoughts, or to know that His ways are tremendously higher than mine (Isaiah 55:8-9), not because I am a whining quitter. There were times when I thought it would be easier to be the kind of waffler that never completed anything, but I would be miserable if I had that ability. I had to learn to combat these 'moods' of mine, by immersing myself in the word. I cannot emphasize how important it is to study the Bible even when you do not feel like it.

One day, I was invited to a social for singles and I talked with several young ladies who could understand the tug between my natural desires and spiritual responsibilities that everyone must deal with on this walk with God. One attractive female in particular, told me that she found it difficult to date Christian men when she desired to be married, and thus had not had a relationship with a man in about ten years. She looked no older than about 30 or 32, but the ten years part nearly blew me away. I felt that I could surely wait a few more months, because I had let God know that it would not take even another year for me to straighten up and follow Him, so that I could be blessed (with a mate).

She spoke of how depressed she had become, so much so that it was difficult for her to get out of bed. She understood the loneliness, the longing, the bitterness, everything I had experienced over a period of about two years before God began to prune me. I did not exchange phone numbers with her, or become her friend, but that brief meeting was enough to inspire me to hold on and believe God for the mate He has already chosen for me.

Keeping the faith can be difficult, but when you continue to keep God's word, it is easy to believe that God will awesomely bless you. As Psalm 84:11 declares, "No good thing will He [God] withhold from those who walk uprightly." As long as you live according to God's principles, you can expect to be exceedingly and abundantly blessed. When you pray daily, you will eventually become more confident that you will receive all that you petitioned God for, despite what satan tries to tell you otherwise.

God I appreciate the fact that I can count on you to be faithful to your word.

"God is not a man that he should lie, nor a son of man that He should repent.

Has he said and will He not do?

Or has He spoken and will He not make it good?"

(Numbers 23:19)

Thank you for turning my distress into opportunities to rejoice and to praise you!

"You have turned for me my mourning into dancing;

You have put off my sackcloth and clothed me with gladness,

to the end that my glory may sing praise to You and not be silent.

O Lord my God, I will give thanks to You forever."

(Psalm 30:11-12)

Heavenly Father, my faith is rooted in your sovereignty and not my circumstances or desires.

Ashan R. Hampton

> *I will always "Have faith in God."*
>
> *(Mark 11:22)*

> *And because you never change, never lie and are faithful to*
> *your word,*
> *I know that you have heard and answered all my prayers.*
> *You have calmed my fears with the strength of your word.*
> *"Now this is the confidence that we have in Him, that if we*
> *ask anything*
> *according to His will, He hears us.*

> *And if we know that He hears us, whatever we ask,*
> *we know that we have the petitions that we have asked of*
> *Him."*
> *(I John 5:14-15)*
> *Amen.*

Chapter 13

❧

DISCERNING MATES FROM MACKS

Beware of false prophets, who come to you in sheep's clothing, but inwardly they are ravenous wolves. You will know them by their fruits.
(Matthew 7:15)

I had almost convinced myself that I could not afford the $70 registration and gas money it would take to drive to and from my hometown where the reunion was to take place. Because I had been excited all year long about attending and visiting with old friends, I said, "God, handle my finances because I'm going!" Before I left, I got my eyebrows waxed and a French manicure all for only $10. I took my car to Jiffy Lube for an oil change and hit the road expecting great things to occur on this trip.

When I entered the first event of our three days of reunion activities, no one recognized me, until I pointed to my nametag. Since high school, I had exchanged nerdy glasses for contacts and had developed a sense of personal style. I secretly enjoyed being the hit of the reunion. Popular guys who had not paid much attention to me in high school complimented me on how nice I looked. During the course of the evening, someone introduced me to a tall, handsome guy that had played basketball on our championship team. Our paths had not crossed until this first night of the reunion.

We spent the next five days getting to know one another, hanging out with family and friends; his family. Because I thought this guy was a potential mate, I praised God for sending me exactly what I wanted. A spiritual, intelligent, tall, dark and handsome man! During all five of these days, Jesus was my best friend. I could not thank or praise Him enough. When we both returned to Atlanta, and this guy asked me out again, I danced around my apartment, just so pleased that God had finally answered my prayer for a mate.

Then, after about a month of hanging out on the weekends and talking on the telephone during the week, as with all my past dating experiences during the two years prior, he stopped calling. I waited patiently for an amazing eight days for him to call, but he did not. I did not even write him off as a lost cause like I would have done before, because I had every reason to believe God had arranged for us to meet and mate, so I tried hard not to return to those old worldly devices I wrote about in "Attitude Adjustment."

Maybe he was busy? Surely he was not rejecting me? I did not want to jump to any erroneous conclusions, so I called a good married friend of mine in Texas to assist me in figuring out this conundrum. Because we have like minds, she suggested I show up at his church just to casually say hello, since I had already attended with him on two prior occasions. I told her that I had already thought of doing that, but refused to pursue a man of God in that way. Did I mention he was a very knowledgeable, on fire minister?

Well, my womanly wiles got the best of me. I drove forty-five minutes out of my way to briefly appear in his congregation just to leave before the benediction. I figured if something was truly supposed to happen between us, then he would call me later that night of the ninth day. Instead, he called at 7: 30 a.m. on the tenth day and asked if I had come to his church. I said yes, and gave a lame

excuse, not a lie, about why I could not stay until the end of service.

He apologized for having taken so long to call me back. At this point,

I was more convinced than ever that we would have a relationship.

For another month, we talked here and there, but we always had

two hour, intensely interesting conversations about the Bible, God

and life whenever we did talk. When my friend from Texas called

again to check in, I told her that although I had not seen him in a

month, we continued to be in touch. She was a bit concerned about

this long absence of physical contact, as was I, but we did not

deliberate this matter. We both were just looking forward to what

would become of the friendship this minister and I had developed.

When October rolled around, I got a bit too antsy about not

knowing where things stood between this guy and me. I thought I

heard the spirit say not to give up on him, but it was difficult to

believe he was the man for me when he had ceased to act like it. One

fateful Saturday night in October, after about four days of not

speaking, I called him with the intentions of finding out if God had told him I was the one. After asking a few key questions, I discovered that God had not told him I was the one. I was disheartened and confused, because I felt foolish about misinterpreting the situation. I was once again in a pit of doubtful mess. I had attributed my ability to hear from God to this relationship developing into a marriage, which now seemed a soiled, broken fantasy. I felt really, really bad, but before I hung up in feigned contentment, he prayed for me. At that moment, I needed that prayer like none before.

Earlier, before he prayed, he had asked me to tell him what I wanted from God, but I refused to say it, so I knew it was the spirit who was telling him what to intercede for me about. He gave me a word from God. He told me that God wanted to bring me into new, deeper depths with Him and be present in my life like never before. I cried. Partly because I had become so discouraged and needed the sweet sentiments of that prayer, and quite honestly, partly because I assumed I was not ready to be the wife of a minister. As a result, I convinced myself that I would have to let go of this one and allow some other more spiritual woman to have him.

Ashan R. Hampton

This time, I was all set to call it quits and I meant it. I let the devil have a good time for a few minutes in my mind. The enemy said, *"If God had anointed you to work in the ministry then you would have seen evidence of it long ago. See, God set you up with this guy, had you practically picking out a wedding dress, and then snatched him from you. You don't need a minister anyway, because you are not operating in spiritual gifts like a man of God needs. You might as well run down guys in the street, and just do whatever your flesh desires with them, because this spiritual mate stuff and waiting on God is not going to work for you. A year from now, in the new millennium, all of your friends will have already gotten married, and you'll continue to watch the rest of the world get married on that show you watch on the TLC network. You'll be some dried up old maid (at 29), still waiting for God to move in your life."*

These destructive thoughts are what psychologists call "negative self-talk," but Christians recognize this as an example of satan's attack on the human mind. The devil had a good time all right. For half a day, I felt like I had messed up God's plans for this relationship. Then an amazing thing happened. Through the tears and grief, I felt compelled to pick up a book called, *The Christian's Secret of a Happy Life* by Hannah Whitall Smith, which was first published in 1870. This small book ministered to every feeling of doubt and regression I had been experiencing.

Slowly, like a plane building up for take off, I realized that I had not fouled God's plan for my life. He had not told me that I was not good enough for that minister. Right then, I realized that I had to continue to seek God and to fervently study the Bible in preparation to move further in my relationship with Christ. I brushed myself off and vehemently swore that satan would never get me to listen to his horrible lies again.

I came back into the peace of God and declared, "Well Lord, I cannot see your ways right now, but even if my minister friend was indeed designed to be someone else's mate, you will just have to send me someone twice as powerful, twice as intelligent, twice as tall, and twice as good looking, because I am prepared to wrestle heaven and earth for this and everything else I have asked of you."

This was not an insolent remark. I believe God likes it when you get a little feisty in your commitment to Him. Hebrews 4:16 tells us to come boldly before the throne of grace. By allowing myself to give in to moments of depression, I had in a sense wavered in my faith. In doing so, I weakened my defense against satan's attacks. God knows that in my heart of hearts, I believe Him, and do not want to quit the journey to my individual promised land. Despite the occasional failings of the flesh, God always honors the intentions of a clean and committed heart.

MATE OR MACK?

It has been a little over a year since I first wrote about my experience with the minister. Since then I have learned many valuable lessons about men and 'church folk.' After I relayed my experience to a close female friend, she recalled a situation that had left a friend of hers devastated after four years of waiting for a young minister to marry her. In my naiveté, I never expected for a Christian man to intentionally or unintentionally break a sister's heart in that way. People date and break up all the time and Christians are just people, but there are certain behaviors that parishioners should not have to deal with in the church. Having multiple dating partners scattered throughout the congregation is one.

For example, another female friend of mine who lives in Atlanta recently relayed to me the story of the ugly man at her church that she foolishly allowed herself to date, despite her initial misgivings. In short, she felt he tried to play her with another woman in the congregation he had supposedly stopped seeing a while before meeting her. I responded on cue with the requisite, "Girl, no he did not's," but in my mind, I chuckled at the idea of an <u>ugly</u> man trying to play Mack Daddy in the Lord's house!

Unfortunately, many women who populate the church pews are easily hurt and made vulnerable to the advances of men they perceive to be Christians. In fact, many women expect to find their husbands somewhere in their congregation. As a result, cunning men can rack up as many hearts or notches on their belts as they desire. Oh yes, unfortunately many women engage in "sanctified sex" with men they think are "saved." Too many people within the body of Christ are walking around with pieces of several individuals' hearts. As a result, I have included this section to help women arm themselves against seemingly Christian men who still have worldly intentions toward them, and to properly discern between potential mates, macks and friends.

HOW CAN I TELL IF HE IS THE ONE?

"If any of you lacks wisdom, let him ask of God, who gives to all liberally and without reproach, and it will be given to him" (James 1:5). First of all, women need to be bold enough to ask a guy the right questions. I have found that men will honestly answer my questions if I make it safe for them to do so. For example, if a man knows that you are extremely sensitive, or prone to violence, he might try to withhold his true feelings for you, out of fear of hurting you, or being hurt by you. As a general rule of thumb, if a man is not demonstrating interest toward you, then he does not want you. If he verbally tells you that he wants a relationship with you, but never

calls you again, then he has decided that he does not want you in that way. If a man goes three or four days without calling you, then he does not want you. I don't care how busy he says he is.

Basically, if a man shows no interest in you, or stops doing so, then he does not want you. Men know whom they want to date and marry. Some of them are smoother at breaking the news to women than others, but women must realize that if a man really wants them, then he will <u>consistently</u> make that known. Women can tell when a man wants to separate from them. The proverbial writing is always on the wall. No amount of prayer or crying can make a man want you if in his heart he has decided against it. Yes, some women do acquire men by these and other forms of manipulation, but the relationships always have problems in the end. Why should a woman waste time praying that God will make a particular man want her? What a pyrrhic victory for her if she in fact does get this man interested in her. Personally, I do not want God to make a man want me. Instead, I want to receive the man whose heart has already been prepared for me. So rule #1 in discerning if a man is your potential partner is to honestly assess his interest in you. If he is not interested, then he is not the man for you, and waiting for him to possibly change his mind is foolish!

A MAN SHOULD DESIRE YOU

"I am my beloved's, and his desire is toward me" (Song of Solomon 7:10). Sometimes when women desire a man, they forget that he must in turn desire them in the same manner. Jacob worked fourteen years to marry Rachel, but the years seemed as days to him. Men will pull out all the stops to have a relationship with you, if they truly desire you.

A MAN SHOULD PURSUE YOU

Many who address groups of singles use Proverbs 18: 22 "He who finds a wife finds a good thing" to biblically prove that a man should pursue a woman. Over the years, several books have been written to tell women how to be caught. These books were controversial because they countered the feminist doctrine that taught women to be the aggressors. Life is about balance and the Christian life is about allowing God to bring that balance into your life. I personally do not think that I should avoid initiating a conversation with a man; however, I will not ask him out! After the experiences I have had with men outside and inside the church, the next man I meet will be my husband and he will definitely have to go to great lengths to chase and court me!

A MAN SHOULD TREAT YOU AS A SISTER

"Do not rebuke an older man, but exhort him as a father, younger men as brothers, older women as mothers, younger women as sisters with all purity" (I Timothy 5:1-2). I jokingly told a friend that I personally did not want a man that I am interested in to start calling me "Sis." However, this verse explains how using that terminology will help a man keep his intentions toward you pure. It is difficult for most people to envision having improper relationships with immediate family members. Therefore, when a man treats you as a sister, he will avoid speaking or acting toward you in a salacious

manner. However, a man should never use the intentions of this verse to avoid or stop having a relationship with you.

A MAN SHOULD RESPECT AND PRACTICE CELIBACY

"It is good for a man not to touch a woman" (I Corinthians 7:1). The spiritual consequences of fornication have been discussed in detail in previous chapters. However, the Bill Clinton/ Monica Lewinski scandal has greatly challenged societal definitions of sex. Basically, there are other ways to receive sexual pleasure without having intercourse, but an enlightened Christian man will not suggest any of those alternatives to you. Oh, people support those alternatives with persuasive arguments, but if a man is serious about relating to you spiritually, in all purity, then he will not ask to come to your apartment to spend time with you, especially at late hours. And he will certainly not even casually mention those sexual alternatives to you either!

A MAN SHOULD BE WILLING TO COURT YOU

How many relationships where you were the aggressor were successful? If the relationship ended, or was unprofitable when you tried to maintain it, then that was not a successful relationship. Men like doing things for women, because they feel useful when they are able to please a woman with their actions. Likewise, a good man will want to take you to dinner, buy you flowers, or take out the garbage for no other reason than to gain your approval by making you smile. A selfish man will want you to do something for him in return out of fear that he will be taken advantage of, but a man who truly knows God is able to give from his heart, knowing that God is the strength of his heart. In Ezekiel 16, God speaks of how he wooed and cared for the children of Israel as a man does a new bride. Notice how God provided for His bride so tenderly and lavishly that she became a shining beauty.

> "And when I passed by and saw you again, you were
> old enough to be married. So I wrapped my cloak

around you to cover your nakedness and declared my

marriage vows. I made a covenant with you, says the

Sovereign Lord, and you became mine. (Ezekiel 16:8

NLT)

And so you were made beautiful with gold and silver.

Your clothes were made of fine linen and were

beautifully embroidered. You ate the finest foods -

fine flour, honey and olive oil - and became more

beautiful than ever. You looked like a queen, and so

you were!" (Ezekiel 16:13 NLT)

These scriptures do not suggest that a woman should manipulate

a man into caring for her. Instead, they clearly demonstrate the extent

to which a man in love will provide for his woman. If a man does not

show a tender willingness to attend to your needs during courtship,

then this will not change on the wedding day. God wants us to

perceive ourselves as being the queens he has created us to be, and to

expect the best behavior from men at all times, whether we are

dating them for marriage or not.

A MAN SHOULD BE WILLING TO SERVE YOU

"Now Jacob loved Rachel; so he said, "I will serve you seven years for Rachel your younger daughter" (Genesis 29:18). Just as Jacob was willing to work for seven years to obtain Rachel's hand in marriage, Boaz was more than willing to serve as Ruth's kinsman redeemer. He allowed her to reap generously of his fields and agreed to marry her. Boaz was willing to serve Ruth in a way that was beneficial to her. As a result, he was blessed with a beautiful young wife and a son, Obed, who propagated the lineage of Jesus Christ. A balanced man will not take the verses that tell women to submit to their husbands out of context and coerce them into fulfilling his needs while disregarding theirs. Instead, he should practice the type of service Peter describes in the following verse. "Offer hospitality to one another without grumbling. Each one should use whatever gift he has received to serve others, faithfully administering God's grace in its various forms" (I Peter 4:9-10 NIV).

209

CLAIMING HIM WON'T WORK

The "claiming" phenomenon that has swept through the body of Christ has grown grossly out of hand. It skews the essence of true prayer by presenting prayer as a means to demand things of God. Prayer certainly is the language of those who are in need of something that only God can supply. And God has certainly given us the ability to ask of Him what we will and to expect that He will grant our petitions, under certain conditions. (See John 14:13-14 and I John 5:14-15).

"Claiming," however is materialistic and manipulative in nature. Underneath this cloaked doctrine of exerting your faith in God lies the dangerous notion that God is a servant at your disposal to grant everything your heart desires. We must remember that <u>we</u> are the servants and God is the master. We are slaves to His righteousness because He bought us at a high price from the prince of this world. How then can a slave boldly demand anything of his master? How can a court jester demand houses, money or land from the King?

Likewise, we do not have the right to demand anything of God, and God's demands of us rest in peace and unselfishness.

Many people who teach or participate in 'claiming' often petition God for material items, and then exert their faith in receiving it. They say things like, "I need a new car, so I <u>claimed</u> that Cadillac Sedan Deville out at Parker Cadillac. I'm tired of driving Toyotas;" or "Somebody else outbid me on that house, but I <u>claimed</u> it, so it is mine."

The focus on this "calling things that be not as though they are" farce is on self. How many people have ever 'claimed' something for someone else that was important, but abstract, like peace or good health? I have never heard the phrase 'claiming' used in this unselfish, non-material manner. Many people who claim things have also been taught that their tithes must be paid up before they can make requests of God. This type of teaching breeds the ignoble practice of paying for a blessing, or giving tithes as a means to manipulate God into providing material goods to the tither.

Manipulation is a form of coercive control. This type of control verges upon witchcraft. God will not move upon misinterpretations of His word and spiritual principles, or out of emotional coercion from the believer.

Unfortunately, some single women have moved from claiming cars, houses and jobs to claiming men! Some have even tried to claim another woman's husband. Frederick Price dedicated a booklet to this topic because of the problems this "claiming a mate" phenomenon caused in his church.

A male friend of mine told me that several women from his church told him of dreams they had of him (from God of course) to motivate him to begin a relationship with them. Is this not outright coercion? I imagine that these women had already 'claimed' him before speaking to him. My friend, however, did not marry any of those women, so what does that say about their 'claiming' prayers?

Why can't you claim a man and expect God to give him to you? First, this is unbalanced. Instead of praying that God will <u>make</u> someone desire you, you should be praying for wisdom; the wisdom to discern whom your God given mate truly is. James 1:5 admonishes us to pray for this type of divine wisdom.

Secondly, God will not override a person's free will, or their right to make choices for their lives. God saw Adam and Eve choose to eat of the forbidden tree, but He did not step in and force them to obey the rules of the Garden. Likewise, God will not step into your romantic situation and force a guy you have your hooks in to marry you.

Because we often desire things according to our flesh, it is dangerous to choose something and pray that God will give it to you. He just might give you that fine man, with two little kids, who is just in a bad situation right now, but then you will have to deal with the consequences of your asking out of ignorance. It is better to pray for your thoughts to be aligned with God's thoughts about your life, rather than to 'claim' something that might not be best for you.

Before I became spiritually enlightened on this matter, I 'claimed' that the guy with the Lexus would call me again, and he did. However, no relationship resulted from that. I am genuinely thankful for this. In hindsight, I am glad that God did not give me half the stuff, or men I had prayed to get! I have found it best to ask God to spiritually reveal to me the truth about various aspects of my life than to go demanding or asking for stuff half-cocked!

ASK GOD

We should always seek God for the answers to life's dilemmas. He might not reveal the answers to our prayers the way we would like, but if we are prayerful and sensitive to the Holy Spirit, then we will know which choices to make. I personally do not believe that God will allow us to miss the mate He has chosen for us, but it is still our right to refuse His first choice. With regard to recognizing the man we are to marry, I think we will receive a gentle, inner urging of the Spirit, not necessarily the bells, whistles and firecrackers that some attest to. This recognition will not be one sided, because the man's spirit will be as equally drawn to you. Attempting to explain falling in love is like trying to define God. In both cases, once you experience them for yourself, you will just know it!

Lord, I will not harbor any bitterness or resentment against men

who have intentionally or unintentionally hurt me.

Instead, I bless their paths and pray that they will find peace in you.

Holy Spirit, remind me that it is better to put my trust in God than in man

when I am tempted to think badly of men, relationships or situations that have occurred within the body of Christ.

I pray that I might be able to see them with innocent, loving eyes as you do.

Thank you for keeping my heart safe and pure against the evil devices that seek to soil it. In the name of Jesus I thank you for your peace.

Amen.

Chapter 14

❧

DON'T GET MACKED

Having a form of Godliness, but denying the power
thereof:
from such turn away. For of this sort are they which
creep in houses,
and lead captive silly women laden with sins, led
away with divers lusts.
(II Timothy 3:5-6)

In the last chapter, I broached a subject that many would rather

not talk about - dating, or sexual activity in the church. Few people

want to address it, because it would be difficult to do so without

indicting the church leadership, as well as the congregation.

I added this section, however, because I in no way want anyone

to think that I place blame solely on the men. On the contrary, there

are many prurient, sexually driven, silly women who intentionally

seduce men within church—theirs and other surrounding churches in the city, in some cases! We see these women; we know these women.

However, I have encountered females with church dating stories, ranging from mild to extreme, who knowingly or unknowingly conduct themselves in a manner that sets them up to be victims of Mack Daddies in and outside of church, but because this book addresses Christian women in particular, I will focus on the activity that occurs in what is supposed to be the Lord's House, a holy sanctuary devoid of worldly issues.

All kinds of people are entering church doors these days. The ones who really need to be there, actually. Former gang members, convicts, addicts, prostitutes, dope dealers, homosexuals, lesbians, satanists, witches—all the people your parents probably tried to shelter you from, if you were raised in a conservative, relatively drama free family. These people, however, still need to be delivered from some aspects of their former lifestyles. Likewise, there are many men and women who have been promoted to the pulpits and other forms of church leadership who are still dealing with the vestiges of lust, or a promiscuous past. Now they are ministers; now they want to get married, and now they are looking at you, and you are looking at them, and satan still sees all of that leftover lust just swirling around between the two of you. The enemy then seizes this opportunity to tempt and pervert the lonely, the celibate and the longing.

So, is that man in the pulpit or your Sunday School class interested in knowing you as a potential mate, or as a sex partner? Now the game begins. Men have a way of manipulating women into tipping their hand, to clearly see what lies beneath all that Sunday induced holiness most women try hard to shield themselves behind while in church. There are some women who can be deemed silly who begin to do all kinds of things at this point that will later make them victims of the man's innate sexual desire, and unwittingly obscure their potential as future wives.

Below is a list of helpful hints that will assist women in guarding their hearts and spirits against the ill intentions of men they might encounter in church. These bits of wisdom address detrimental behaviors Christian women should absolutely avoid, because they actually deter men from establishing meaningful relationships with them, whether they be of friendship, or marriage. Beyond that, there are just some retarded things Christian women do that need to be stopped anyway, in the name of self-esteem, self-respect, and the mighty name of Jesus!

1. Remember that a 'saved' man, a minister or other male officer in a church is still a man—subject to all the failings and lusts of any old regular man on the street.

2. Do not offer attractive men in church your phone number. Remember that the man should pursue the woman. (But a harmless smile never hurt anybody!)

3. Do not invite men to your apartment thinking that they will be perfect gentlemen. (There is not that much Bible study in the world!)

4. Do not accept an invitation to a man's apartment thinking that you all will just watch TV.

5. Wearing tight or low cut clothing to church will make men notice you, especially from the pulpit, who will proposition you for sex, not marriage.

6. Do not buy a man a gift for any reason, especially to get into his good graces, or to give yourself an edge over the other female competition.

7. Cooking excessively for church functions or other get togethers will not make that man consider you as a potential wife, if it is not already in his heart to do so.

8. Do not talk to male officials of the church alone or in locked, enclosed spaces.

9. Do not entertain the advances of a married man. (Regardless of how much he likes you better than his wife.)

10. Do not pretend to need prayer or counseling to get next to the pastor or other male leaders in the church. (Remember what happened to Jezebel.)

11. Do not date a guy who has dated another female in your church. (Leave all that drama to Jerry Springer.)

12. Know that some men view single mothers as easy sexual prey, so beware, and make sure their intentions are pure.

13. If you pop over to a guy's house unannounced, don't get mad at what you encounter. (Men always have women stashed somewhere.)

14. Do not allow a man you have decided against as a potential partner to attend family functions, or hang out with your parents.

15. Avoid men of other religious beliefs—even those fine Muslims!

16. If you have sex with a man in your church, understand that every other man knows about it, and expect to be approached by another man who wants to 'get to know you.'

17. If you wear sleeveless outfits, sundresses, toe rings, ankle bracelets and open toe shoes that slap against your feet,

then expect to get approached for sex, especially in the summer. (All that slapping around reminds a guy of every sweaty, freaky thing he has ever done with a woman.)

18. Remember that women with tattoos and body piercings are still considered loose, rebellious women, regardless of the nature of the tattoo. (This is still America.)

19. Do not give a man money, excessive gifts, or access to your credit cards. (Don't be a Judge Judy casualty!)

20. Why do a man's laundry or clean his house if you are not his wife? There is not that much generosity in the world. (Besides, he'll invite the other woman over to benefit from all of your domestic skills.)

21. Beware of men who give you pet names, or shower you with terms of endearment too soon. (This is psycho behavior.)

22. Beware of men who have little to no contact with their family and have one too many 'spiritual' mothers or 'sisters' in Christ.

23. Getting a man—unsaved or backslidden—in church will not make him spiritual or Christ-centered. (You'll just have a heathen on the pew next to you.)

24. Do not continue to call a man who has stopped calling you. He has probably done so for a good reason, so save yourself, let him go and move on with God.

25. Beware of married men who want you to befriend them and their wives. Why would a married couple need single, female friends? (Freakier things have happened in the Lord's House!)

At some point, I might just tour the country gleaning tips like these from other women who have learned a thing or two about sex, dating and establishing relationships with men in church.

The key to not becoming a victim to a mack, however, is to listen to the Holy Spirit; to those uneasy feelings that keep you from moving forward with a particular action. But if you are living carnally, given to the lusts of the flesh and the eyes, then you will have to learn the hard way, because you are not in a position to hear clearly from God.

I have encountered women who swear they are so together, so spiritual, who would never allow a man to mistreat them, who are so celibate and waiting on the Lord for their divine mate, who have either in the past, or are preparing to be engulfed in the drama of a relationship gone awry, especially if they are involved in internet chatting and dating, which is on a swift upsurge amongst eligible African-American women.

Take heed to the above admonitions, and to those of friends or spiritual laborers who call your attention to beliefs, behaviors, or personality characteristics they have observed within you that might make you susceptible to temptation or deception. None of us should ever overestimate our holiness, or strength to counter all of satan's tactics, because he is formulating some different ones, in the 21st century, that we are not totally equipped for, which involve male/female relationships, marriages, sex and the internet that are beginning to manifest themselves in our world, and amongst people we know in sundry, increasingly bizarre ways. Remember to consistently and vigilantly pray without ceasing, so that this evil will not come nigh your dwelling.

A WORD ON SOULISH PRAYERS

In the church dating scene, some well intentioned people often weave curses around themselves and their 'love' interests. How so if we are all children of light and not of darkness? First remember that everyone in church is not there to worship or to grow spiritually. Some are there to expand their business, find a mate, molest children, take advantage of the elderly, or to conduct reconnaissance missions for occult or satanic organizations.

With regard to soulish prayers, however, other Christians are just ignorant about the principles of blessings and curses, and the power of words to bring both to pass, and as a result, they say wrong things in conversation and in their prayers, without realizing the consequences of their words. Whether intentional or unintentional, some people might be hindering you from connecting with your mate by launching selfish, controlling prayers against you. In his book, *Sharpen Your Discernment*, Roberts Liardon briefly but compellingly discusses the nature of soulish prayers. He writes, "Sometimes well meaning but very ignorant Christians send demonic activity into your life by their soulish prayers for you. Soulish prayers stem from a personal desire over and above the desire of God. If you're praying your personal, lustful desires to affect the life of another person, you're practicing witchcraft."[iii]

These prayers often take the form of 'claiming' prayers and can occur as innocently as this:

"Lord, the new minister at our church is just the kind of man I've been looking for. Please fix it so that he will notice me in church, talk to me, date me and fall madly in love with me, so that we can be the spiritual couple you have called us to be. Amen."

"Lord, I just know that the man in my Bible study class is the one for me. Please let the situation between him and his wife come to a peaceful end, so that we can become a Godly family and ministry team. Amen."

These are examples of more obvious selfish prayers that can be detrimental to you and the person included in them. However, what about prayers that others say they are praying for you in regards to your mate? Do you think everyone who tells you this has the ability to pray healthy, Holy Spirit inspired prayers for you in this area of your life? Consider the following example:

"Lord, my daughter is over thirty and single, but she desires to be married. Lord, just send her a saved man, with a college education, a little money in the bank, no kids, no mental illnesses; don't let him be like the other men she has dated. Let him be honest and filled with the Holy Ghost. Thank you that it is done. Amen."

What is wrong with this prayer? It sounds like the basic "Lord let me have grandkids" kind of prayer that many parents have no doubt prayed for their children, but especially their daughters. Still don't know what's wrong with this prayer?

This person has limited the hand of God by rattling off their personal preferences for the daughter's mate, instead of praying that the daughter be led by the Holy Spirit to prepare her life to receive a mate, and to discern <u>God's</u> first choice in a mate for her. We might be presented with one or several good options for a mate, but the Holy Spirit will help you to choose according to God's will for your life, if you are sensitive to His voice and promptings.

Another good source to read about the issues of soulish talk and soulish prayers is Derek Prince's *Blessing or Curse: You Can Choose.* In plain, easy to read language, he dynamically uses the scriptures to explain these principles. After reading these books, I realized that I had tried to manipulate the situation I discussed previously between me and the young minister, with my words and actions. I also discovered that the poor dear had been the victim of other hindering, claiming prayers. Although I could not remember what I said in this regard, I immediately repented anyway, and prayed that any curses I ignorantly launched against him would be rendered of no effect, according to the power of the blood of Jesus Christ to destroy satan's evil intentions. I also prayed that I would not be adversely affected by the soulish prayers of others who were intentionally or unintentionally hindering me from connecting with the mate God has chosen for me, as well.

Become more knowledgeable of the power of words, the word of God and the principles of blessings and curses, then ask the Holy Spirit to reveal to you if vain, hindering words have been sent forth to work on your behalf. Remember that Jesus became a curse for us on the cross, to defeat the devil's work in our lives and in the world, so curses and vain words cannot destroy a believer, but they can surely oppress, confuse and bedevil you, until you learn how to protect yourself against the influence of witchcraft! As Derek Prince concludes, "The power of soulish prayer is both real and dangerous. The result it produces is not a blessing, but a curse."[iv]

> *Lord, open my eyes and ears that I might see any snare that has been set for me, or that I might have unknowingly set for myself.*

Shield me from the deception and temptation that is so pervasive in the church

by intensifying my desire to live righteously and acceptably in the eyes of my Lord and Savior.

Teach me the tactics of the enemy, so that I will not be ignorant of the devices that satan might use to make me stumble in my faith walk with God.

Lord flood your sanctuary—my body and my place of worship—with your Holy Spirit to cleanse your house from the filth, perversity and moral compromise that the body of Christ has opened the door of the flesh to.

Make us all your holy bride, without spot, wrinkle, or blemish, filled with the hope and the expectation of your second coming.

In the name of Jesus, I thank you that it is done.
Amen.

Chapter 15

❧

SET YOUR AFFECTIONS ON THINGS ABOVE

For where your treasure is, there your heart will be also. (Matthew 6:2)

By recognizing that Christ did indeed want a closer relationship with me, He made it easy for me to understand how to go about functioning within this new relationship. Because I truly desired a mate and had read numerous relationship books, I understood what my role should be in a natural relationship with a man. In the process of translating this natural knowledge into spiritual practice, God had to prune, or clear away the obstructions in my mind and heart that precluded me from fully functioning according to His will.

As I look back, parts of this process were humorous, depressing and confusing, but no matter how distressing it became, every incident that occurred along the way was crucial to my understanding of my place with God as a single woman. Now that I am a bit more comfortable in my relationship with Jesus Christ, I understand that I must be fashioned into a vessel, without defect, that can be filled continuously with the Holy Spirit.

I wish I could tell you that a fabulous man appeared on my front door step with a big red bow and a tag that read, "From God with Love," but this has not happened yet. Instead something even more wonderful happened. Remember the minister I mentioned in "Discerning Mates and Macks"? A few months after he had stopped calling me, I called him. I stopped being salty with him for not calling me long enough to discuss some pressing spiritual issues. After about two hours, he startled me with this question. "Do you really want the Holy Spirit, Ashan?" He was talking about the Baptism of the Holy Spirit as evidenced by speaking in tongues. I replied affirmatively. "I can have one of our female altar workers pray with you tomorrow and you'll be speaking in tongues before you leave!"

At this point in my spiritual journey, I had made great gains in Christ, but I had no firepower to keep going higher and further with

God. I wanted something more and had prayed to receive more of the presence of God before having this discussion with my friend. I had reached a point where I needed more spiritual resources to climb the next mountain in my life. My mother said I was like a Chevette trying to make it up a steep hill, but I needed Cadillac power to make it. Up to this point, I was on a spiritual roller coaster, up and down with God, though more up than down.

Believe it or not, I hesitated when he offered me the best gift he could possibly have offered anyone. I said, "Let me sleep on it, and if I call you in the morning before church, then you will know that I am coming to your church." Was that not insane of me to hesitate? That experience was like having someone say, "I can give you the best love of your life right now; all you have to do is say yes," but when confronted with getting what I had been seeking, I was reluctant to go for it. I made the decision to receive within the next five minutes, but I waited until the morning to call him back.

That Sunday morning, March 12, 2000, I was preparing to leave for church with nervous anticipation. I got dressed in my lilac Kasper suit, nice jewelry, hair nicely styled, but I called my mother before calling my friend and heading for his church. I told my mother that I was going to receive the Baptism of the Holy Spirit and asked how she felt about that. "How do I feel? I feel great!" I expressed my concerns about not knowing the woman my friend had in mind to pray for me. My mother prayed for me before I hung up the phone. As soon as I put the phone back on the hook, I immediately fell to the floor, on my knees at first, then literally on my face. I cried and praised God violently; up and down, between raised arms and bowing to the floor.

I felt so much pressure in my throat I thought I was going to choke if whatever it was did not get out. My throat felt like it had swollen to three times its normal size. I lifted my mouth straight to the ceiling between gasps, and when I did, foreign sounds came forth. I just relaxed and let it come forth. I was praising God in my spirit language! After a while, I just lay in child's pose, an extreme bowed position, sweaty and spent in my fine designer suit. I began to giggle. God had come to see about me in a big way and I laughed with joy, until I realized how irritated my throat was, but it cleared after a few moments.

I composed myself, reapplied my makeup and adjusted my hair before calling my friend as I had promised. I did not tell him what had just happened. Instead, I drove to his church and let the sister explain to me about the Holy Spirit. (I did not tell her I had been teaching a class on the Gifts and Fruit of the Holy Spirit.) It was like Holy Ghost round two, because the exact experience I had just had in my apartment was being repeated. Once again the pressure in my throat rose and I began to speak again. I joined their congregation for worship service as a new woman.

After that experience, I entered a spiritual battle like I had never known before, but now, exactly one year later, I am concluding this book as a strong, forever changed woman of God. I have more peace than I have ever had in my life. For the first time, I am not concerned about my life or my future, because my faith rests completely in God. I have entered a new dimension of spiritual truth that many Christians do not understand, and will not, until they are totally surrendered to God. God has opened doors for me that I had been trying to enter on my own a year ago. My future is bright and I am genuinely excited about how God is going to use my life for His glory.

More importantly, I have totally gotten over the man drama! I no longer fear that my family and friends will never see me get married. Instead, I am just waiting patiently on God's timing. At this point, however, my focus is on my relationship with Christ. By making Him a true, consistent priority, I am convinced that all areas of my life will harmonize in a most excellent way by the power of the Holy Spirit.

The true meaning of "Setting Your Affections on Things Above" is to desire nothing or anyone but Christ, Christ and more of Christ, and to be willing to let go of everything to gain Him. Once you have gotten to the point where you are not bound to things of the past, God will create a new thing in you. This new thing will be built upon his love, Holy Spirit and spiritual laws instead of the trappings of satan's world. I pray that everyone finds the courage to lay down her old life to find new and eternal life in Christ. Matthew 6:33 gives us the formula to finding rest and life in Christ. "But seek first the kingdom of God and His righteousness, and all these things shall be added to you." What does it really mean to seek the kingdom of God first?

SEEK THE KINGDOM OF GOD

In order to know more about God and His plan for you as a follower of Jesus Christ, you must make a definite break with the world. Why? Because satan is the prince of this world and it operates according to sin, greed and destruction. However, since we are human, we must use the world's resources to live, but we are not supposed to be caught up in its snare. We are not supposed to think, act, or look like people who have not given their lives to Christ.

In order to be made new in Christ, we must give up everything that we did not consult God about. We must also release everything that will hinder our relationship with Christ. This does not mean that you are to become unbalanced and quit your job, isolate your friends that curse, or become a nun. It means that when you earnestly get tired of your present, powerless, loveless life and pray for God to change you, that you must allow the Holy Spirit to clean out whatever He needs to in order to give you a fresh start in Christ.

Seeking God's kingdom means that you want spiritual truth, love, abiding faith, eternal life and all the gifts that God wants to give you. It means that you must stop praying for a new car, a better job, a husband, or whatever material things you thought would make your life better. You have to make up your mind to focus on God and not on the material goods of the world. Quite simply, seeking God first means that you have decided that you love Christ more than anything in this world, and that you are willing to do whatever it takes to have your life reflect that love.

Jesus said that whoever tries to maintain the life they have created in the world will lose it; however, those who lose their lives for His sake will gain eternal life. "For whosoever will save his life shall lose it: but whosoever will lose his life for my sake, the same shall save it" (Luke 9:24 KJV). Although God's way is straight, narrow and bittersweet, it brings sweetness to your earthly life and eternal reward in heaven. You can only gain life in Christ by giving up your attachments to the world.

In his classic book, *The Release of the Spirit*, Watchman Nee characterizes life in Christ in the following words. "Brokenness is the way of blessing, the way of fragrance, the way of fruitfulness, but it is also a path sprinkled with blood."ᵛ Brokenness means that God has penetrated all of the pain and desires you accumulated in the world, and is breaking that hard shell to expose His spirit that is within your heart. The shell of a seed has to be broken before the life giving roots can be released from it. Likewise, God must break the shell of your flesh in order to release the spiritual roots and fruit He has sown inside of you. This process does not feel good. In fact, it creates wounds that only the Holy Spirit can heal.

This is the process that creates blood, according to Watchman Nee. In the words of A. W. Tozer, the veil that separates us from Christ is made of flesh, and when that veil is severed, it hurts us because it contains the living matter of our lives. Once the veil is torn, however, there is nothing hindering full fellowship with Christ. A wound must hurt before it can heal. Therefore, we can expect our hearts to be broken, so that those old wounds can be healed at the root. God in His infinite mercy and love gives us the grace to pass through this process without the memory of the pain; much like a woman who endures the travail and pain of labor, but forgets it once the baby is in her arms.

SEEK HIS RIGHTEOUSNESS

"For if ye live after the flesh, ye shall die: but if ye through the Spirit do mortify the deeds of the body, ye shall live" (Romans 8:17 KJV). You have got to give it up! All of those things that you do or have in your possession that do not glorify God must go! These things will be different for everyone, but let me give you a rapid-fire list of potential hindrances to you serving a holy God.

Sex partners

Cybersex

Immoral Internet sites

Chatting with strangers on web sites, date lines, etc.

Music with lustful or unclean lyrics

Food that makes you sick or fat

An excessive amount of sugar or sweets

Clubs, provocative club clothes

Masturbation

Sex toys

Pornographic books, pictures or videos

Cable movie channels (e. g. HBO, Cinemax, Showtime, etc.)

Condoms and lubrication products

All types of alcohol (including wine, or wine coolers)

Food, coffee or dessert with alcohol in it

Boyfriends you have had sex with

Guy friends who want to have sex with you

Guys you have met in clubs or bars

Navel, nipple, facial, genital or other body piercings

Tattoos or the desire to have a tattoo

Some of that hair weave, false nails or other body embellishments

(Maybe we can keep the push-up bras?)

Sexy underwear (Trust me.)

Provocative dancing

Live-in relationships (Shacking)

Affairs, or excessive contact with married men

Pride, bad tempers, etc., etc., etc.

Why would you need to release some of that hair weave or false nails? Because many women focus too much time and energy on the maintenance of their hair and nails. If you sleep in odd positions so as not to mess up your hair, or freak out when you break a nail, then your focus is on those objects and not Christ. Let's be real. Some of us do not attend church regularly, but will never miss a hair appointment! This is idolatry. Idolatry does not only apply to those who worship false Gods, or have altars with crazy looking figurines and statues in their homes. Idolatry also means vanity or excessive devotion to something or someone. There are numerous scriptures in which God strictly forbids and warns believers about indulging in these practices.

What is wrong with body piercings or tattoos? There is a long occult history surrounding these practices that is much too complicated to even mention. Push-up bras? I personally wear them, but not so that people or men will admire my chest. Some women honestly wear bras or clothing that accentuate their breasts, because they want to be seen as sexually attractive. This motive is contrary to wanting others to see Christ in your life.

I believe that Christ wants women to be sexy and attractive, but the source has to be His Holy Spirit, not a short skirt, or skin tight workout clothes. God's spirit makes a woman beautiful from the inside out and all people, not just men, will be attracted to the beauty of God's spirit within you. Quite frankly, when you have refrained from sex for long periods of time, all that sexual energy combined with the Holy Spirit makes women of God irresistible. So if a brother whispers a passing compliment to you during church, it does not automatically mean that he has a demon of lust in his flesh, but that

God is caring for you in a most excellent way!

I cannot overemphasize how important it is to commit to a lifestyle of holiness. God is a holy God and He will never recognize or encourage anything that satisfies the flesh. Those who allow the flesh, or their carnal appetites to rule their lives cannot please God (Romans 8:8). The trick of the devil is to make you think that you are bound to your flesh and sin, and that you will always succumb to temptation. The other is to make you think that people will think you are weird or that old friends will not accept you, and your new lifestyle of holiness. Some of those friends don't need to be in your life anyway!

I can attest to the fact that although your basic personality will remain the same and God will not make you weird, that your mind, heart and soul will undergo an amazing transformation. I have not abandoned all of my old friends, but more than one has told me that I sound different now. More than one old guy friend has told me that I seem more relaxed and less man hungry! The Holy Spirit will make precious and abiding changes in your life. If you remain committed to Christ, your life will be bittersweet, but you will experience more sweet than bitter.

ALL THESE THINGS WILL BE ADDED UNTO YOU

What do you want out of life? What do you really want from God? If you desire good things and your motives are pure, then God will grant those desires of your heart. God will grant those things that He has ordained you to have that will bring health and life to you. However, eye has not seen nor has ear heard all of the wonderful blessings that God has in store for us!

Some people believe that God does not want us to be rich, or that He will not encourage our professional success or dreams. Yes, He will. There are too many scriptural examples of people whom God has made successful in the eyes of the world. The condition is that you always keep God and His word first; then and only then will your life be made prosperous.

For example, God knows that I really want to be out of debt and He has begun to open doors for me that will bring financial peace. Instead of praying for more money to get more stuff, I prayed to be released from the bondage of debt, because I cannot focus completely on God if I am worried about bills and money. This financial peace will also facilitate a good courtship and marriage with my future husband. What man really wants to be with a broke woman, or to attach himself to all of her debts? I do not want to have to work to pay off my husband's past debts, so God is making me ready for my debt-free man who will then be able to afford more trips to Paris and Jamaica. (See how God's system works?)

When you commit to following God's spiritual laws, He will be faithful to provide above and beyond your needs. Because He is your husband and loves you dearly, He will even throw in gifts you did not even ask for, just because. This is the type of relationship I expect to have with God and my husband. A marriage relationship should be a reflection of God's love for both partners. Despite what the media says, this kind of relationship is available to all of His followers who desire it and commit to making God the center of that union.

ON THE OTHER SIDE OF THE FIRE

I have made it to the other side of the fire. On the other side of pain, confusion and dissatisfaction is unspeakable peace and true relationship with Christ. What did it cost me to get here? Everything! Everything in the world I held dear had to be totally surrendered to God, including my <u>desire</u> to be married. Why? So that He could give me something much bigger and better than I could have imagined three years ago when I first began to write this book. I recently made what I thought was a simple comment during a single's conference seminar. I told the group what the Holy Spirit had revealed to me about God's generous nature.

While studying the account of Hannah, Samuel's mother, in I Samuel, the spirit showed me that by offering her only son - that she had prayed so long and hard for - to serve God in the temple, that she was sacrificing her very heart's desire to God. This was a major sacrifice, because she had been pronounced barren before giving birth, so Hannah had no guarantee that she would have other children. However, God honored her, and her willingness to release what she valued most in life, by blessing her with three additional sons and two daughters, "for the loan which [was] lent to the Lord" (I Samuel 2:20 KJV).

Therefore, in requiring me to surrender my desire to be married, my professional desires, etc., God is not withholding His gifts from me. Instead, He is multiplying what I have given Him, and making the manifestation of those desires more spectacular than I could have ever imagined. And He will release all of those precious gifts to me in His timing, if I continue to obey Him. The group began to applaud before I completely finished, not because I was so great, but obviously, that was a word many of them needed to hear.

PRESSING ONWARD

I now conclude this book at my present point in life, as a young woman, still single, still desiring a mate, but who has become increasingly more clear about God's perfect will for her life. I continue daily to release my thoughts and ways to receive God's thoughts and ways. We learn "precept upon precept, line upon line; here a little there a little," (Isaiah 28:10) sometimes in a slow progression rather than by leaps and bounds.

But as verse nine from the above passage in Isaiah declares, "Whom should he teach knowledge? And whom shall he make to understand doctrine? Them that are weaned from the milk, and drawn from the breasts." In other words, Christians who are spiritually mature and do not faint at the least little attack of satan will apprehend true knowledge of God. However, you cannot mature without first having a very personal, thriving relationship with Jesus Christ.

I truly hope that my experiences and pitfalls have encouraged you to focus more on developing a relationship with Jesus Christ, and treating Him as your first husband, so that He can teach you to share your love of Him with the very best mate He has chosen for you on earth, and to everyone you encounter on a daily basis who need to see Jesus in someone who professes to be a Christian. May God's will for you be done on earth as it is in heaven. As Psalm 34:2 says, "Our souls shall make their boast in the Lord: the humble shall hear of it and be glad." God Bless!

A FINAL NOTE ON BEING 30 AND SINGLE IN THE 21ST CENTURY

Although I have edited this book many, many times over the past year, I completed the basic manuscript at age 29. Now that I have obtained victory over the hormonally induced drama about turning 30, and have become comfortable with confessing my true age to people, I have just turned 31! I have read through this manuscript as you have - as a spectator, peeking in on the life of a single woman who was struggling to live the holy life that Christ demands of us in a world that does not encourage righteousness. We are constantly surrounded by sex and the various lusts of the flesh, not only in the world in the process of daily living, but unfortunately in our churches as well.

It has been eight months since the September 11th terrorist tragedy occurred, but Americans are still reeling from the fall out; particularly, the spiritual fall out. Now, more than ever, people want a relationship with a higher power, so questions and iconoclastic attacks against religion, especially Christianity, are fueling discussions about spirituality in schools, breakrooms, around water coolers, and places that had once discouraged the mention of God, regardless of the religion. People are looking for answers, but not just any answers.

People are seeking spiritual truth, but unfortunately, they are having a difficult time finding it amongst those who profess to be Christians, because so much moral compromise has been allowed to infiltrate the body of Christ. We listen to Yolanda Adams on the local R & B radio station, and then sing that same song on Sunday mornings during church service. Likewise, Donnie McClurkin's popular song, "We Fall Down" has been remixed for play in secular dance clubs across the country. People are hungering for those who can show what their relationship with Christ has borne them; signs, wonders, gifts and fruit. Likewise, God is looking for people who will make a complete break from secular living and live the <u>uncompromised</u> gospel of Christ daily and wholeheartedly.

IT WAS NOT ALL ABOUT GETTING A HUSBAND

This chronicle of my pitfalls on the road to spiritual peace was not just about getting clear with God so that He would be more inclined to send me a husband. The experiences I have shared are what constitute true spiritual development. Shedding old beliefs and behaviors that we have accumulated in the world in order to live for Christ more fully is often a painful, funny, ineffable, tripped out journey, for lack of a better word, that ultimately results in clarity about the scriptures and Christian life. The situation that catapults an individual on her own quest for spiritual truth is different for everyone, but relationships, especially bad ones, usually prompt women to seek a more meaningful, abiding fellowship with God more so than any other tragedy.

Statistics show that over half the American population consists of single households, whether by divorce, death, or choice. There are many women, as well as men who are dying to get married, and who are feverishly praying to God for a mate. Unfortunately, many women are not seeking God's guidance in their mating and dating activity, which is resulting in increased deaths among women due to domestic violence, or crimes of passion. Black women and women in general, are silently slipping from this earth at the hands of angry ex-boyfriends or husbands. Every time I hear a news report about one of these incidents, I immediately think about the thousands of women who are in fear of having the same murderous fate befall them, and the many incidents that go unreported.

Perhaps if another Christian had been bold enough to open their personal lives to talk honestly and boldly about God and satan's ideas on relationships, then maybe they could have avoided involvement with those murderous or otherwise abusive men. My overall purpose in exposing my soul in print is to tell every single woman I can that life alone with Christ is much better than one with half a man, or one that they are sharing, or fruitlessly pursuing, or coercing to establish a relationship with her.

You can actually obtain peace in singlehood, even with the pressures of raising children alone, yet still believe that God will allow you to experience love and marriage according to His thoughts and spiritual laws before Christ returns to reclaim the earth! Jesus said that He came that we might have life and to have it more abundantly. This abundant life also includes marriage and children, but the Lord is calling us to love Him first, with a single heart so that the earthly items that constitute the abundant life will not become necessities, or obsessions, but items to be enjoyed as the rightful inheritance of a believer in Christ, the one true God.

On a lighter note, it seems I have become the single woman of choice for friends who know someone who is seeking a good single woman who is "doing something" with her life. Friends and relatives of mine know of brother-in-laws, colleagues, sons or complete strangers who are seeking a single woman to talk to. Sometimes, when I walk in churches, I feel as if I am on single woman alert, where women are assessing how much competition I might produce in the man war, and older married men are wondering where I was when they were looking to get hitched. To be honest, I am so ready to meet my spiritual partner, so that I can be somewhat shielded from the looks of angst, appraisal and referral services of those who think that 30 is a little too old for a woman to have not been married at least once!

I was listening to a female, new age guru (don't stone me) who was lecturing on romantic relationships. She said that the whole idea of finding one person to fulfill your life for the rest of your life was an illusion from satan and a trick to obscure the eternal, abiding presence of God's love that cannot be compartmentalized into specific kinds of love for specific kinds of people, under certain conditions. Only God can fulfill your every need, and the search for one person in the world to do that for you is futile.

When the Holy Spirit affirmed that truth in my spirit, I took a deep breath and relaxed. I was able to talk and hang out with attractive guys without creating man fantasies about future relationships with them, or devising ways to remain in touch with them afterward. The emotional wounds I carried about men and relationships had been officially healed and I rejoiced! When I think of all the tears I shed to get to this point, I feel like the lame that Jesus made to walk, the blind he made to see and the deaf he made to hear! I have received a bona fide healing that I had to walk out and work for, through the process of time, not one that was magically zapped into me.

This type of newness in Christ is available to every woman, regardless of what her most pressing issues are, if not marriage and the single life. So be inspired to seek the easy yoke and the freedom in Him that Christ promises us in the scriptures. Move, breathe in Him and taste the divine sweetness of this newness of life.

"If ye then be risen with Christ, seek those things which are above, where Christ sitteth on the right hand of God.
Set your affection on things above, not on things of the earth."
(Colossians 3:1-2 KJV)

PRAYERS FOR THE SINGLE SOUL

...to heal the brokenhearted, to preach deliverance to the captives, ...to set at liberty them that are bruised. Luke 4:18 KJV

As Presented At The End Of Each Chapter In

Set Your Affections On Things Above

PRAYER #1

**For your Maker is your husband, The Lord of hosts is His name...
(Isaiah 54:5)**

Dear God, In the name of Jesus, I come before

you today with an open heart, asking that you

fill it with the love you have for me.

I have been so hurt and disappointed in past

relationships

that did not fulfill my needs for companionship or

love

like I thought they would.

Your word states that you have loved me with an

everlasting love, and I pray to enter into your divine,

loving presence right now to be healed and made

whole

by your Spirit that is always surrounding me.

May I feel and always be reminded of the divine love

you have for me.

In Jesus' name I thank God that is done,

Amen.

PRAYER #2

**He shall be like a tree planted by the rivers of water,
That brings forth its fruit in its season;
Whose leaf also shall not wither;
And whatever he does shall prosper. (Psalms 1:3)**

Dear God,

I come before your divine throne of grace and mercy,

asking that my mind and concept of time be released

to that of Christ's.

Forgive me for the things I have done and wrong

words of faithlessness

I have spoken in trying to make things occur in my life

according to my timing and not God's.

Your word says that you know the thoughts you think

toward me, and that they are of peace.

Help me to accept the wonderful plan you have

designed for me,

that will unfold in the fullness of your divine timing,

flowing with the blessings you surely have in store for

me.

In Jesus' name I pray and thank you that it is done.

Amen.

PRAYER #3

Draw near to God, and he will draw near to you. (James 4:8)

Heavenly Father,

I thank you and praise you for the enlightenment that

I am receiving concerning my life and relationship

with you.

Lord, I am committed to following your ways and to

having

your spirit released in my life.

Therefore, I pray for the strength to release my

attachment

to everything in my life that is hindering me from

drawing closer to you.

In Jesus' precious name, I pray and thank God that it

is done.

Amen.

PRAYER #4

Therefore a man shall leave his father and mother and be joined to his wife, and they shall become one flesh. (Genesis 2:24)

Dear God, thank you so much for revealing to me

the characteristics of a Godly woman.

I recognize that in my own strength I can never become

a virtuous woman, but by your Holy Spirit, I can become

the Godly woman and wife you desire for me to be.

Release me from the fear of remaining unmarried

and of incompatibility with the husband you have

chosen for me.

I want to always remember that you are a good God

and that you

give only good gifts to your children.

I acknowledge my desires to be married as a

willingness

to receive this precious, spiritual gift that will not be withheld,

but freely given to me by your hands in due and divine time.

In Jesus' name I thank you that it is done.

Amen.

PRAYER #5

For your Maker is your husband,
The Lord of hosts is His name;
And your Redeemer is the Holy One of Israel;
He is called the God of the whole earth. **(Isaiah 54:5)**

Thank You Lord for revealing your true intentions for
marriage to me.

Thank you Holy Spirit for showing me the areas of my
heart

and lifestyle that are not yet prepared for marriage.

I will honor my singleness as an opportunity to
prepare to minister

to the wonderful man you have chosen for me, so that

I will be a beautiful

and welcomed addition to his relationship with you,

Heavenly Father.

Thank you that it is done.

Amen.

PRAYER #6

For the lips of an immoral woman drip honey,
And her mouth is smoother than oil;
But in the end she is bitter as wormwood,
Sharp as a two-edged sword.
Her feet go down to death,
Her steps lay hold of hell. (Proverbs 5:3-5)

Dear Holy Spirit,

Help me to understand God's will for my sex life and sexual desires.

I have not always considered God's feelings about my sexual expression, but I sincerely want to align my lifestyle with the word of God.

Please help me to do that.

I admit right now that giving up this sinful act that has brought me pleasure in the past will be extremely difficult for me emotionally and psychologically, but I am committed to releasing everything in my life that is not pleasing to God.

I want to stand within the grace and holy presence of God without any hidden sin, guilt, shame or hypocrisy.

I truly want my life to reflect the obedience and love I have for Christ.

Thank you that it is done.

Amen.

PRAYER #7

*Do not be unequally yoked together with unbelievers.
For what fellowship has righteousness with
lawlessness?
And what communion has light with darkness?
(II Corinthians 6:14)*

Lord, your word says that you will show me the path
of life;

in your presence there is fullness of joy and at your
right hand are pleasures

for evermore (Psalm 16:11).

Strengthen my heart that I may weather the
disappointments in life without sinning against you
God. Send your sweet Holy Spirit to comfort me, to
dry my tears when loneliness and distress creep upon
me.

I know that you are a faithful God and you always
honor your word.

If I delight myself in you, then you will grant this
desire of my heart for a mate.

In the meantime, give me the strength to remain faithful to you.

Thank you for creating an escape from temptation
whenever I falter and consider succumbing to sinful pleasures,
or make wrong decisions.

Thank you for your Love, Grace and Mercy!
Amen.

PRAYER #8

For whom the Lord loves, He corrects. (Psalm 3:12)

Dear God,

Search my heart and reveal to me any hidden sins that I need to confess.

I am ready to submit my life and thoughts to your will and word.

Holy Spirit, bring to my attention any behaviors that do not please God,

so that I can openly and honestly petition for your help to change.

There are areas of disobedience in my life that I want to faithfully surrender to

You, Heavenly Father.

Thank you for providing me with this opportunity to turn from my carnal ways and commit my life wholly to the Lord.

In the name of Jesus I thank you that it is done.

Amen.

PRAYER #9

By this My father is glorified, that you bear much fruit;
so you will be My disciples." (John 15:8)

O Lord, you have searched me and you know me.

You know when I sit and when I rise; you perceive my

thoughts from afar.

You discern my going out and my lying down; you

are familiar with all my ways.

Before a word is on my tongue you know it

completely, O Lord.

You hem me in - behind and before; you have laid

your hand upon me.

Such knowledge is too wonderful for me, too lofty for

me to attain.

(Psalm 139:1-6 NIV)

Thank you for searching me Lord and finding me

good!

Amen.

PRAYER #10

*Therefore, if anyone is in Christ, he is a new creation;
old things have passed away; behold, all things have
become new.*
(II Corinthians 5:17)

Thank you Lord that your word is a balm to my soul;

a love letter engrafted upon my heart.

Surely in my sweet communion with you,

I hear these words dance lightly in my ear:

"How beautiful you are, my beloved, how beautiful!

Your eyes behind your veil are like doves.

You are so beautiful, my beloved, so perfect in every

part.

You are like a private garden, my treasure, my bride!

You are like a spring that no one else can drink from, a

fountain of my own.

You are like a lovely orchard bearing precious fruit,

with the rarest of perfumes: nard and saffron, calamus

and cinnamon, myrrh and aloes, perfume from every

incense tree, and every other lovely spice.

You are a garden fountain, a well of living water, as refreshing as the streams from the Lebanon mountains." (Song of Solomon 4:1, 7, 12-15 NLT) Amen.

PRAYER #11

Jesus said to him, "You shall love the Lord God with all your heart,
with all your soul, and with all your mind."
(Matthew 22:37)

Heavenly Father,

Thank you for being everything to me, even the love of my life.

It is amazing how you reveal yourself to me differently

in relation to the events of my life.

I have seen you act as a friend, a father, a counselor, and a gentle lover;

So many expressions of your personality I could name.

You have fulfilled so many needs in my life, yet remained the same.

What an amazing, glorious, living God I serve!

All praises be to God almighty!

Amen.

PRAYER #12

Now may the God of hope fill you with all joy and peace in believing, that you may abound in hope by the power of the Holy Spirit. (Romans 15:13)

God I appreciate the fact that I can count on you to be

faithful to your word.

"God is not a man that he should lie, nor a son of man

that He should repent.

Has he said and will He not do?

Or has He spoken and will He not make it good?"

(Numbers 23:19)

Thank you for turning my distress into opportunities

to rejoice and to praise you!

"You have turned for me my mourning into dancing;

You have put off my sackcloth and clothed me with

gladness,

to the end that my glory may sing praise to You and

not be silent.

O Lord my God, I will give thanks to You forever."

(Psalm 30:11-12)

Heavenly Father, my faith is rooted in your sovereignty

and not my circumstances or desires.

I will always "Have faith in God."

(Mark 11:22)

And because you never change, never lie and are faithful to your word,

I know that you have heard and answered all my prayers.

You have calmed my fears with the strength of your word.

"Now this is the confidence that we have in Him, that if we ask anything

according to His will, He hears us.

And if we know that He hears us, whatever we ask,

we know that we have the petitions that we have asked of Him."

(I John 5:14-15)

Amen.

PRAYER #13

Beware of false prophets, who come to you in sheep's clothing, but inwardly they are ravenous wolves. You will know them by their fruits. (Matthew 7:15)

Lord, I will not harbor any bitterness or resentment against men

who have intentionally or unintentionally hurt me.

Instead, I bless their paths and pray that they will find peace in you.

Holy Spirit, remind me that it is better to put my trust in God than in man

when I am tempted to think badly of men, relationships or situations that have occurred within the body of Christ.

I pray that I might be able to see them with innocent, loving eyes as you do.

Thank you for keeping my heart safe and pure against the evil devices that seek to soil it. In the name of Jesus I thank you for your peace.

Amen.

PRAYER #14

Having a form of Godliness, but denying the power thereof:
from such turn away. For of this sort are they which creep in houses,
and lead captive silly women laden with sins, led away with divers lusts. (II Timothy 3:5-6)

Lord, open my eyes and ears that I might see any snare that has been set for me, or that I might have unknowingly set for myself.

Shield me from the deception and temptation that is so pervasive in the church
by intensifying my desire to live righteously and acceptably in the eyes of my Lord and Savior.

Teach me the tactics of the enemy, so that I will not be ignorant of the devices that satan might use to make me stumble in my faith walk with God.

Lord flood your sanctuary—my body and my place of worship—with your Holy Spirit to cleanse your house from the filth, perversity and moral compromise that the body of Christ has opened the door of the flesh to.

Make us all your holy bride, without spot, wrinkle, or blemish, filled with the hope and the expectation of your second coming.

In the name of Jesus, I thank you that it is done.
Amen.

PRAYER #15

For where your treasure is, there your heart will be also.
(Matthew 6:2)

Lord I thank you for demonstrating such love for me.
Thank you

for taking the ordinances, the sins that were against me and nailing

them to the cross, to render satan, sin and death of no

effect in my life.

During my journey to peace and wholeness, you extended such grace and

mercy to me, as I struggled to understand my pain, my desires, my healing.

Thank you for giving me a new heart and cleansing my soul of all unrighteous

thoughts, past wounds and abuse, so I now know love, the love of Christ, of

which there is only one and no higher love; for God is love, and he who

dwells in love dwells in God, the only one true and living God.

I bless the paths of all the men who entered my life to

teach me lessons,

some good, some painful, because they brought me to

my knees, and into

the arms of the one who loves everything about me—

all that I am, have been

and will become.

Thank you Jesus for being my first husband, my

friend, my healer, my heart.

Thank you for this peace.

Thank you for this everlasting love.

And so it is. Amen.

About the Author

Ashan R. Hampton, author of the novel, *Like She Knows Single*, has worked as an English Instructor, most notably at Morehouse College in Atlanta, Georgia, for five years. She is a graduate of the Donaghey Scholars Program at the University of Arkansas at Little Rock where she earned a B. A. in English. She received a Master's in English from the University of Central Arkansas and was briefly enrolled in a humanities doctoral program at Clark Atlanta University. In 2000-2001, she was invited to the highly competitive Scholars-in-Residence faculty research program sponsored by the Faculty Resource Network at New York University. She is currently a professional writer, an active freelancer and independent scholar.

Visit her website http://www.singlesoul.com for updates on future writings and author tours.